How to Recycle Husbands Every 10 Years

I0520080

eParte Publishers
P.O. Box 1111
Portage, Michigan 49081
or email: minettesummers@gmail.com

Published in collaboration with
Fortitude Graphic Design and Printing & Season Press LLC.
Design and layout by Sean Hollins
Consultant editor, Sonya Bernard-Hollins

Printed in the United States of America

ISBN 978-0-9887387-0-6

First Edition

10 9 8 7 6 5 4 3 2 1

In loving memory
to my mother, Mrs. Ella.P.

ACKNOWLEDGMENTS

I would like to thank my husband, family, and friends for your support. Lenore and Keva, you were my inspiration for writing this book. Thank you Charlene, Darby, Debra, Janice, Joyce, Karen, Michelle, and Shireen for your unwavering support and encouragement. A special thanks to the editors at 2 Chicks and A Manuscript, LLC. And I want to acknowledge the most extraordinary man in my life, my Dad (Wil), and his extraordinary wife (Dollie). I love you. T.A.P. Thank you for posing.

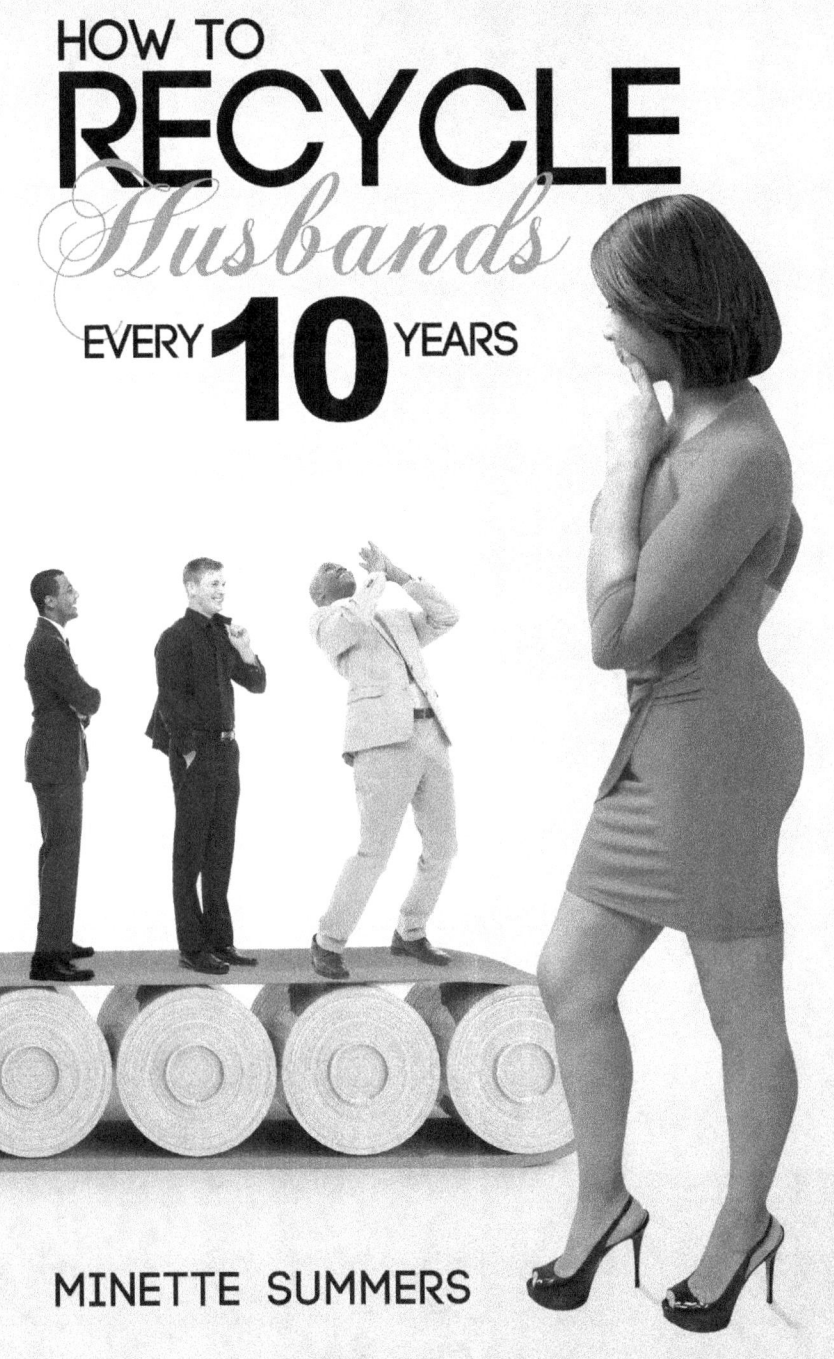

HOW TO
RECYCLE
Husbands
EVERY **10** YEARS

MINETTE SUMMERS

INTRODUCTION

How to Recycle Husbands Every 10 Years is a fiction story about an unconventional approach towards marriage. It demonstrates common behaviors that could have you walking down the aisle, not once, not twice, but three or more times during your life.

If you are thinking of recycling your husband, and you have the attitude, stamina, finances, and medication to do so, this guide is for you. You may also have a slight advantage if you are a modest drinker, smoker, or have a therapist on speed dial. For those of you who have a heart condition, extremely high blood pressure, or a serious illness, recycling is not recommended.

Before you learn how to recycle husbands, the assessment below will determine if you have the necessary psychological profile. Answer each question below with either a 'Yes' or 'No'.

1. Do you believe in true love?
2. Are you a thrill seeker?
3. Do you forgive people easily?
4. Can you keep a secret?
5. Are you attractive to anyone other than your mother?
6. Do you make friends easily?
7. When you win an argument with your spouse, do you follow-up with the silent treatment to drive your point home?
8. Are you able to function on five hours of sleep?
9. Have you had a physical within the last 12 months?
10. Do you have (and use) a gym membership?
11. Can you afford a therapist, liposuction, or Botox?
12. Are you thinking about recycling your husband?

If you answered, 'YES' to seven or more questions, CONGRATULATIONS! You qualify as a candidate to recycle husbands every 10 years! If you answered 'NO' to six or more questions, recycling husbands is not for you, so pass the book to your girlfriend who is dancing with glee over the fact that she qualified.

RECYCLING HUSBANDS
Part One

Chapter 1

"**S**o many men, so little time," I whispered as I approached the hottest nightclub in town. There was excitement in the voices of those who lined up and down the sidewalk, dressed in their party clothes, and waited eagerly to get in.

As I stood in front of the entrance of the glitzy club, a mean looking 260-pound bouncer who had to be almost seven-feet tall, folded his muscular arms and gave his best power stance. I scanned the long line and decided that, rather than wait an hour to get in, I would see if a little flirting could get me by the bouncer. In my skin-tight red spaghetti-strapped dress, and four-inch stiletto heels, I stepped out of line and walked towards the bouncer. The pronounced sway of my hips moved to the beat of the muffled music coming from inside. As planned, the bouncer's gaze zoomed in. We made eye contact.

His eyes followed each step like a trained marksman who watched his prey. I smiled. A tiny smile appeared on his face and he moved over and opened the door to let me in. I winked as I passed by and entered the lobby, which was decorated with a beautiful crystal chandelier hanging in the center of the room. The carpet was a plush royal red framed with giant gold leaves.

The walls were covered with floor-to-ceiling elaborately beveled mirrors. Two cashiers wore black tuxedos, and collected the money. Everyone looked fashionably elegant.

When three couples got in line to get their hand stamped to enter, I tucked my black clutch under my arm and fell in line behind them. As I looked around for my girlfriend, the guy in front of me said, "Girl! You fine! What's your name?"

"Ashley," I said as I tried not to stare at his digital glow-in-the-dark watch.

"Ashley, Um Umm Ummm…That's a pretty name." He looked me up and down as if I was a menu item.

"Thank you," I replied politely, and at the same time, eased back a step to prevent him from drooling on me.

"Hey man," a male attendant interrupted him, "You going in?"

"Yeah man, I'm in." He held his fist out as the attendant stamped his hand and gestured with his head to go inside.

"I'll see you again, Miss Ashley," he said as he disappeared behind the tall royal blue velvet curtain.

"Hey Beautiful," the attendant said to me. He then gave me a big hug.

"James? I thought that was you!" I hugged him back.

"How's it going?"

"I'm doing good. Looks like life is treating you well," I said as I reached over and squeezed his muscular biceps.

"It's good seeing you again Ash." His eyes did a quick full body inspection of me. He wanted to say more but realized there were others behind me who waited to get in. He kept his eyes on me as he opened the curtain to let me into the club.

I walked by swinging my hips to the rhythm of the beat. Inside, the atmosphere was inviting and intoxicating. I looked around and saw mirrored disco balls reflecting light off of diamonds, mirrors, gold chains, and Jheri curls. The dance floor was packed with couples who grinded to the slow beat of the Isley Brothers' "For the Love of You."

I eased my way through the crowd and headed to a long beautifully carved cherry bar in the back. There was one seat left. I passed by many handsome men who had dates on their arms. Some of them stole looks of me out the corner of their eye as I pretended not to notice.

On queue, the deejay changed the music to a faster beat. The aisle opened up and a big burly guy who held a drink in each hand, barreled his way down the aisle towards me. I jumped out of the way, lost my balance, and fell backwards into a crowd. On my way down, a hand grabbed my arm and pulled me back to my feet with so much force I ended up in his arms.

Our eyes locked as he held me. It felt good in his arms, and I did not struggle to get free. Before I could come to my senses he asked in a smooth baritone voice, "Are you okay?"

I stared at him with a blank expression, hoping the moment would never end. His head tilted to one side like he was checking me for brain damage. His steel gray eyes mesmerized me. His eyes narrowed and before he said another word, I blurted out, "Yes, I'm fine. Thank you."

"Not a problem."

He released me, nodded goodbye, and turned around and continued his conversation with his friends. Feeling rejected—a feeling I don't feel very often—I smoothed my dress and walked over to the bar. The tall, slender male bartender stopped washing the glasses and asked what I wanted to drink.

"Red wine please."

"Sweet, dry, or semi-sweet?" he asked, flirting.

"Sweet, please."

"Coming right up!"

I swiveled my chair around and looked for the handsome stranger. *Damn, no sign of him.* Disappointed, I turned back around as the bartender placed the wine on the bar.

"Three dollars," he said tapping his finger.

I opened my purse and handed him a twenty. He moved to take the money and stopped. A hand appeared over my shoulder and gently pressed my wrist down on the bar. I turned around and saw beautiful steel gray eyes. It was the stranger. *He found me! Hallelujah!*

"May I?" he asked.

"Yes you may," I said batting my eyes.

He looked at the bartender, "I got it. And bring me a Hennessy on the rocks please."

Hmmm... Got manners. Check!

He leaned over the guy's shoulder on my left and whispered something in his ear.

Cute butt. Double check!

Within seconds, the guy left and he moved the chair closer and sat down.

Knows how to get people out of his way. Triple check!

"So tell me, pretty lady, do you fall into people often?"

A giggle escaped my lips and I quickly regained my composure.

"Not really," I responded. I took a sip.

"Do you come here often?" His voice was smooth as he leaned his tall muscular body closer to mine and rested his arm over the back of my chair.

"No, I don't. I'm meeting my best friend."

"Is she as beautiful as you?"

"Yes... she is." I blushed. "Are you here with friends?"

"No, I came alone and spotted a few coworkers. That's where you fell into me."

"Ohh... Lucky me." I said slightly embarrassed. I took a big sip. Out of the corner of my eye I saw him canvassing my body, so I decided to give him a better view. I sat my glass down, leaned toward him, and crossed my legs. He watched my dress split open to my thigh, and picked up his glass and said, "Touché."

Checkmate!

His voice dropped to a near whisper. "You have beautiful long legs."

His voice seeped into my body like fire. Beads of sweat popped across my forehead. He smiled. Dimples appeared. I lost my train of thought. I removed the napkin from under my glass, patted my forehead and dried the palm of my hands. I could see him thinking, "She's easy to arouse." *Check!*

I took a cigarette from my purse and placed it suggestively between my lips. *Two can play that game.*

A light appeared out of thin air as he lit my cigarette. I took a long pull and turned away from him and blew the smoke over the girl's head next to me who had also been eyeing the stranger.

"What's your name?" he whispered in my ear as he glided his index finger gently down my back.

I looked at him with bedroom eyes, "My name is..."

"Ashley wake up!" my roommate, Laurie, yelled as she knocked on my bedroom door.

My eyes instantly opened. The stranger vanished.

"Damn, what time is it?" I asked, trying not to sound mad and hoping I did not oversleep.

"Ten after seven," she said dressed in her favorite pink bathrobe with a head full of matching pink foam rollers dangling from her hair. "Time for you to get up so you are not late for work again."

"Thanks for waking me up," I said sarcastically as I watched her fumble through my jewelry box.

"You're welcome," she responded, modeling my gold hoop earrings in the mirror.

Laurie and I had been best friends since fifth grade. We were college roommates, and now share an apartment together. She treats all my possessions as community property, and hers as sole ownership. Even so, I still loved her like a sister.

"Can I borrow these?"

"Yeah. Just don't forget to return them," I said resting my arm over my eyes.

"Okay."

"I dreamed about him."

Laurie closed the jewelry box and turned around. "Him… who?"

"I don't know who." I closed my eyes, and tried desperately to recapture his image.

"Move over," she said with urgency. She pushed my legs back to make room to sit on my bed. "What did he look like?"

I looked at the ceiling and a tiny smile appeared. I took a deep breath, closed my eyes and said, "Tall, muscular, chestnut brown complexion, with piercing steel gray eyes."

"Fine time to be dreaming about another man when you are getting married in two weeks," she quipped.

"I know!" You know I love Tony."

"Yeah, I know, but your subconscious doesn't. It's a sign."

"A sign of what?"

"Maybe Tony is not the one you should be marrying. You know you've had your share of ups and downs."

"Most couples do right before they get married. That's not unusual."

"I hope you're right."

Chapter 2

*T*hirty minutes later, I was stuck in traffic on Interstate 95 near the Baltimore Harbor in Maryland. I turned up the radio, lit a cigarette, and let the memory of my past slip back into my mind. I smiled.

It was the summer of 1980. I was an intern at the Ross & White Accounting Firm located in the heart of downtown Chicago. During those three months, I became great friends with the other interns, Kyle Ayers, Michelle Fetzell, and James Ellwood. They wanted to celebrate our last weekend together in Chicago.

"Ash, this is our last weekend together and we are planning on going out for dinner tomorrow to celebrate. You in?" asked Kyle.

"Well I…I…"

Sensing my hesitation, Kyle interrupted, "If you can't make it tomorrow, let's get together Saturday for lunch."

I had been avoiding getting too close to Kyle on purpose. There was a chemistry between us that I didn't want clouding my judgment. Some days I wondered if he felt the same way because he never crossed the line of respect.

"Okay, Kyle," I said with trepidation, "I'll let you know later."

That day I worked a little later than normal and on my way home, I stopped and picked up Chinese food. By the time I arrived home I was starving. I walked in the door, dropped my purse and keys on the counter, and pressed play on the answering machine.

"Hey Ash, give me a call when you get in." Beep… end of messages.

I opened the carton of beef and broccoli, tore the paper off the chopsticks, and picked up the phone to return Tony's call.

"Hey, Tony," I said answering the phone with a mouth full of food.

"Hey, Baby. How was your day?"

"I had a good day. Worked a little later than normal on an audit. Thank goodness we are almost done. Just imagine, one more week I'll be back home and we will be together forever."

We laughed for a few seconds then Tony cleared his throat.

"Listen Baby. Tomorrow I'll be calling you after midnight."

"Why?"

"I'm going to Red's Sports Bar after work with a couple of guys."

"What guys?" I quipped.

"Don and Jake," he responded firmly.

Don was cool, but Jake was a lady's man and cheated on his girl all the time. Frankly, I didn't understand why she put up with his crap.

"Jake!" I said louder than normal. "You're going out with Jake and you know how I feel about him?"

"Yeah. I know."

"Then why didn't you tell him 'No'?" My grip tightened around the phone and my mouth was right on the mouthpiece.

Tony responded back fast and loud, "Ash, I don't need your approval to go out with my friends. I know you don't like Jake but he's my friend. You are acting like you don't trust me again and I'm not going to argue with you. I'll talk to you later."

The phone went dead.

***

It's Friday morning, payday and everyone is happy. As I sat at my desk applying makeup, I heard, "Good morning." Kyle walked into my office holding two cups of coffee.

"Good morning, Kyle. Is that for me?" I asked with a look of surprise.

"Yes, it is."

"Thank you. That was thoughtful of you."

Kyle was always full of surprises. Monday he brought in bagels; Wednesday, donuts; and today, coffee. I was really going to miss him.

"You're welcome," he responded with a broad smile. "So, are we having dinner tonight?"

"Yes, we are. Where are we going?" I began to blow on my coffee before I took a sip.

"There is a great steak restaurant two blocks from here called Will's Steak and Grill House. We are going to walk over there right after work. I already made a reservation for five-thirty."

"Great, I think I'll have a light lunch so I'll be good and hungry later."

"Cool, I'll see you later."

The rest of the day dragged by. I was the last one to leave the office at 5:30 p.m. and was glad I only had to walk two blocks to the restaurant. The waitress escorted me to the booth where my friends were seated.

"Hey Ash," they say unison.

"Hey guys!"

Kyle slid out of his seat to allow me to sit next to him. I intentionally left enough room between us to avoid touching his body.

"Kyle recommends the prime rib, Michelle is getting a rib-eye, and I'm going with the prime rib," said James with his arm over Michelle's shoulder.

"I love prime rib and I don't need a menu to order that," I said as I folded the menu and placed it back on the table. A few minutes later, the waitress returned with another round of drinks and Kyle had her take a group picture of us with his Kodak camera.

One by one we talked about our lives, and our future plans. Kyle was from Long Island, New York, the oldest of four, and a student at Central State University who loved Jazz. He planned to return to Chicago after he graduated and become a CPA.

James was from Houston, and attended Texas Southern University, and his dream was to get drafted into the NFL. A degree in accounting was his Plan B if he didn't get drafted into the NFL. Michelle was from Newport News, Virginia and attended Hampton University. Her goal was to complete her Master's degree right after graduation and start her own accounting business.

I announced my goal was to become a C.P.A., marry Tony, have three kids, and live happily ever after. We all agreed on how exciting it would be to return home; everyone except Kyle who suddenly became unusually quiet for several minutes.

Three glasses of wine later, we all felt a stronger bond between us. I had loosened up and closed the seat gap between me and Kyle. Kyle paid the entire bill and three hours later, we walked out of the restaurant into the bright downtown city lights.

"Where to next?" asked James.

"Navy Pier," Kyle said pointing in the direction.

It was a beautiful, breezy summer evening. Perfect for a romantic walk. Kyle and I strolled behind Michelle and James who were acting more like lovers than coworkers. Surprised by their behavior, I nudged Kyle in his ribs. He gave me a 'where have you been?' look.

"Well, I don't keep up with who's dating who at the office."

"They've been seeing each other for over a month."

"It all made sense now. No wonder they get along so well at work. They're working on and off the job!" We laughed and Kyle put his arm over my shoulder. I didn't resist.

"Ash, Tony is really lucky to have you. You are beautiful, smart, kind, compassionate, and have a great pair of legs."

I laughed. "Thank you. And you are not so bad yourself. You have a great personality, a great sense of humor, fun to be around, and handsome. I'm surprised you don't have a girlfriend."

His mood changed instantly and he became painfully subdued. With a blank stare he said, "I had a girlfriend… for three years."

It quickly became obvious that what ever happened he was still feeling the pain.

"She loved to shop," he said, "She and her girlfriend Sharon shopped every weekend. One day they were sitting in the car at the mall waiting for the rain to stop. When the rain let up, they got out to run into the mall and were struck by lightning." He stopped and looked at me. "Sandy didn't make it."

Right away, I wished I hadn't asked. "I'm sorry Kyle. I didn't know."

I was glad the atmosphere at the Navy Pier was festive, exciting, and contagious. Minutes passed and the sadness slowly left Kyle. A Caribbean band was playing on steel drums. People were dancing, drinking, and having a good time. Out of compassion, I hugged him. He looked down at me with warm eyes and smiled. We walked down the pier in silence until he heard the sound of a loud boat horn.

"Hey there's a sight-seeing boat docked up ahead. Let's cruise," he said rallying up the group.

"Any time you are ready," James said picking up the pace.

"I am ready," I said.

Twenty minutes later, we were cruising and a cool Lake

Michigan breeze blew through my hair. I leaned back on the railing and focused my gaze on Kyle.

"What would you like to drink?"

He could tell I was a little cold and a drink would definitely warm me up. "I'll have a glass of wine, please."

"Red or white?" he asked walking towards the bar.

"Red, of course."

"I'll be right back," he said.

I looked at my watch. It was 8:45 p.m. I wondered what Tony was doing. I heard Michelle giggling and turned around and saw her hugged up with James like lovebirds. I tried to remember the last time Tony and I did something romantic. My mind came up blank. No wonder I feel like I'm on a date.

"I'm back," Kyle said holding two glasses of wine. "For you my dear," he said bowing like a king presenting a gift to a queen. "And a toast to our last weekend in Chicago. May our paths cross again."

We tapped glasses as I said, "Yes, may our paths cross again."

He kissed me on the lips. I didn't resist.

Chapter 3

*T*he next morning the phone rang four times before I answered. I cleared my throat, "Hello."

"Good morning Miss Rise and Shine. I called you a couple of times last night. Where were you?" Tony asked.

"Morning, Baby. I went out."

"Out where?" he asked with an investigative tone. Tony was a Criminal Justice major and will question me until he gets a satisfactory answer.

"I had dinner with a few coworkers." I made my voice sound as monotone as possible. "It's our last week working together and we celebrated. Sorry I missed your call."

"I don't remember you telling me you were going out."

I faked a yawn long enough to collect my next thought. "I wasn't planning on going, but they kept insisting. No big deal." Not wanting to linger on that subject I asked, "How was your date with Jake and Don?"

"It wasn't a date, smart ass. And we had a good time, drank some beers, watched a few games, threw darts, and that was it."

"Hold on, Baby, someone is calling on the other line. Hello."

"Ash!" Laurie said with urgency. "I saw Tony out with another girl last night."

My heart dropped.

"What!" I shouted. Hold on!" I switched back to the other line.

"Tony! Were you out with another woman last night?" I asked loudly. The froggy monotone voice was gone.

"What! What are you talking about?" His voice escalated over mine.

"Laurie said she saw you out with another woman last night!" My heart pounded hard.

"Now, wait a damn minute Ash. She probably saw me talking to Jake's cousin, Angie. She tagged along with us."

"What did she look like?" I paused to rip into him.

"Hell, I don't remember. Short, short hair, kind of stocky looking." Tony realized he was defending himself and stopped. "Why?"

"Hold on." I pressed the flash button and returned to Laurie. "Laurie, what did she look like?"

"Girrrl… she was short, about 5'2, a little on the heavy side. Had short hair with a bad ass cut, kinda' cute. She had on black pants, black top that had a sexy see-through crochet design in the back. I didn't see a bra strap...and she wasn't sagging either. And…"

"Laurie! You're not making me feel better."

"Okay…okay. She was wearing black shoes, gold hoop earrings, and..."

"I'll call you back."

"Okay."

I switched back to Tony.

"Uh…Baby..."

"What!" he snapped, biting my head off.

I let a few seconds pass. "I'm… sorry."

"Do me a favor Ash. Tell Laurie she needs to mind her damn business!" Click. "Damn!"

***

The internship ended and I returned to Baltimore to a not-to-happy Tony. After convincing him that I was not the insanely jealous type, we moved forward with our relationship. Toward the end of my senior year, I was engaged; and secured a full-time job as an accountant with Ross & White's Baltimore, Maryland division.

Chapter 4

August 7, 1982, a white limousine pulled up in front of St. Theresa's Catholic Church in Silver Spring, Maryland; 12 p.m. sharp. The driver opened the car door and helped the bridesmaids Laurie, Karen, Debra, Pam, and Kathy out the car.

I looked out of the window and admired how beautiful they looked standing shoulder-to-shoulder, holding bouquets of mixed flowers against their teal blue gowns. Having a moment to myself, I closed my eyes, and prayed. My childhood dream was becoming a reality. I was getting married.

After a few moments of silence, I signaled the driver that I was ready. He opened the door. I folded the train over my arm and handed him a bouquet of white roses that held a single red rose in the middle. I grabbed his hand and stepped out wearing a strapless fitted white gown embroidered with tiny pearl beads across the bodice. An attractive elderly lady wearing a light gray suit greeted us on the steps.

"Hello, are you Ashley?"

"Yes, I am."

"My name is Cheryl Farmer, and I will be assisting you today. Welcome, and follow me, please." She escorted us to a Chamber to wait for the guests to arrive.

An hour later, Tony arrived with his groomsmen, Don, Jake, Jeff, Darion, and Reggie. They joined him on the church steps wearing their black tuxedos. They teased Tony and told him they left the Mustang running in the parking lot in case he changed his mind. Their fun was interrupted by a distinguished-looking gentleman who opened the front door.

"This way, Gentlemen." They followed him into the church, down the aisle, and into a chamber behind the altar. He looked at Tony, "Which one is the best man?"

"I am," Don said.

"Hello, I am Mr. Brooks. Remain here with the groom and the rest of you follow me."

The guys followed the gentleman back through the church to a small room next to the bridesmaids. As we waited for the guests to be seated, Laurie chatted incessantly while I zoned out into deep thought. Several minutes later, my thoughts were interrupted when someone knocked lightly on the door. It was my father and Mrs. Farmer. After she gave us instructions on how to proceed she placed her hand gently on top of mine and looked up.

"It's 2:15 and the guests are seated. Are you ready?" she asked with a gentle smile.

I took a deep breath. "Yes."

She smiled. "You look beautiful, and I wish you all best in the world."

She left the room and notified the priest that the wedding could begin. The pianist and soloist took their place at the front left side of the altar. Mr. Brooks opened the chamber door behind the altar, and gestured for Tony and Don to come out and take their place in front of the altar.

Conversations stopped mid-sentence. The soloist gave the

pianist the signal to start playing. She sang, "Ava Maria", and the doors at the back of the church swung open. One by one, the bridesmaids alongside the groomsmen, gracefully walked down the aisle. After the wedding party was in front of the altar, the doors in the back were closed. There was a long pause. Guests grabbed their cameras and waited. The priest nodded to the pianist who started playing the "Wedding March".

The doors opened. The guest gasped with delight and dozens of flashbulbs went off simultaneously and created a strobe-light effect. I took my father's arm as he looked lovingly into my eyes and forced a smile. I could see a little sadness behind his eyes and smiled back, reassuring him that I was happy. I looked at Tony and he smiled and rocked nervously back and forth on his heels until we were face to face.

"Who gives this bride away?" The priest looked at my father.

"I do," my father said. He took my hand, then kissed me gently on my head. "I love you," he whispered and placed my hand in Tony's. He gave Tony a nod of approval and took a seat next to my mother who was wiping tears from her eyes. Twenty minutes later, the priest announced Mr. and Mrs. Tony & Ashley Parks to the congregation.

Chapter 5

*T*ony and I shared a blissful first year of marriage. The first couple of months we were so in love that we overlooked each other's bad habits and idiosyncrasies. But, one early morning trip to the bathroom resulted in me making a splash.

"Tony!" I yelled at the top of my voice. "You forgot to lower the seat!" He smiled and pretended to be asleep. "Tony!"

"Huh, what?" he said muffling his laugh in the pillow.

"The toilet seat! You forgot to lower the toilet seat and I sat down in the water!" I stormed out of the bathroom with a wad of toilet paper wrapped around my hand wiping my butt. Tony started laughing. "It's not funny!" I said standing over him pointing the wad at him. "Will you please lower the seat after you use the bathroom?"

"Okay, Baby," he said laughing.

"It's not funny!" I threw the wad at his head which made him laugh even louder. I jumped on his chest, grabbed a pillow and started beating him over the head with it. "Stop," wham... "Leaving," wham... "The," wham... "Seat," wham…"Up!" wham.

He grabbed my hips and rolled me off to the side laughing. "I'm sorry Honey. Did your butt get wet?"

"Oooo… you make me sick!" I rolled over and turned my back to him. His laughter died down. Five minutes later, I heard a light snore. *What the… How the hell did he fall asleep so fast?*

"Tony… Tony!" I said, loudly.

"Huh…what?"

"You sleep?"

He looked at me and frowned, "I was."

"Oh." I said fluffing my pillow to lie back down.

"What's up, Ash?" he said in his loving 'Honey, Sugar, Baby,' tone.

"Nothing."

"Well since you woke me up, I've got something to say. The next time I'm driving, do me a favor and don't tell me how to drive." He pulled the covers over his head and off of me, as he turned his back towards me.

"I don't tell you how to drive."

"Yes, you do," he said agitated. He sat up to defend himself. "If I'm driving too slow, you tell me to speed up. If I'm driving too fast, you tell me to slow down. If I pull into a parking lot, you tell me where to park. If there's a light rain, you tell me when to turn the wipers on and when to turn them off. If I know where I'm going, you give me directions. I appreciate your input but I don't need it, Honey."

"Oh, I see. It's true confessions time?"

"No, just stop being a backseat driver. It irritates the hell out me."

"So now I irritate you? What else? You may as well get it off your chest."

"Okay." He threw the covers off himself and sat up. "You know how you always leave dishes in the sink until the next day? Why don't you rinse them off and put them in the dishwasher and turn the dishwasher on?"

I was in full defense mode and shot back, "Why don't you put them in the dishwasher if it bothers you that much? And why don't you take the trash out when it's full and running over instead of waiting until Saturday?"

The confession bullet ricocheted back at Tony and he shot back, "And why don't you put your make-up away? It's all over the bathroom counter. I can't even shave with all that crap in front of me!"

"Listen, when you start picking up your clothes, making the bed, washing dishes, doing laundry, and lowering the toilet seat, I will have time to clean off the bathroom counter!"

He unloaded, "I would make the bed in the morning, but your ass is still in it when I leave for work! And speaking of ass... come here wet booty." He grabbed me before I could get out the bed and pulled me into his arms. "See, I told you, you would get mad."

"I'm not mad." I said pouting.

"Then why are you struggling to get free?" He tightened his grip. "Stop fighting wet booty." he said softly.

I relaxed and smiled. He kissed me, and I didn't resist.

Life is good.

Chapter 6

*N*ine months later, on April 20, 1984 at 11:18 a.m. Rachael Maria Parks arrived weighing a healthy 8 pounds 4 ounces. She would bring more joy into our lives than the night she was conceived. Tony took off four weeks from his police duty to enjoy being a new dad and helped me adjust to the day-to-day rhythm of having a newborn baby. Our parents were overjoyed to help out too.

The next three months I spent getting Rachael and myself on a schedule. When she slept, I cleaned. When she was awake, I was consumed by her every demand and loved every minute. Occasionally, I held her in my arms as she slept. The thought of leaving Rachael to return to work tortured me daily.

"How depressing," I uttered as I hugged and kissed her gently on her head.

"What is, Baby?" Tony asked as he walked out of the bathroom sporting a clean shave.

"Going back to work." I stroked Rachael's soft black hair as she slept in my arms.

"Ash, we already had this discussion and we both agreed we need your income to maintain our lifestyle. Look at it this way, the more you work, the more clothes you can buy for Rachael."

I knew Tony was right but it did not make me feel better. "Here, hold Rachael for a minute." I placed her in his arms and reached under the bed and fumbled around for his gift. I grabbed it and pulled it from under the bed.

"Happy Anniversary." I puckered my lips for a kiss. Tony gave me a quick smack on the lips, put Rachael down on the bed, and opened the box.

"Thank you, Baby," he said as he ripped off the paper. Within seconds, he burst out laughing. "How did you know I wanted this gaming system?"

"I overheard you telling Don you couldn't wait for it to come out."

"Really? That's why I love you. You're thoughtful, nosey, and a great wife. And… I got something for you." He pulled a small black velvet box out his back pocket. "Happy Anniversary, Ash."

I grabbed the box out his hand and opened the lid slowly. I gasped and grabbed my chest. "A diamond bracelet! It's beautiful. Thank you! Thank you!" I held out my wrist so he could put it on.

"I know I keep saying this, Ash, but thank you for giving me a beautiful, healthy baby. You are the best mom in the world."

He leaned over and kissed me. "And you're the best husband in the world."

After we smooched a bit, I reminded him that we had reservations that night at our favorite seafood restaurant on the Harbor in two hours, and a reservation at the Renaissance Hotel. His parents had agreed to watch Rachael for the night. In the meantime, I complained about having the hardest time finding anything to wear.

"What are you talking about? You have a closet full of clothes," Tony said.

"Yeah, but I can't fit most of them any more." I felt myself starting to panic and walked over to the closet and started working my way down the left side swishing hanging clothes to the side as if I was in a retail store.

"No…no…no, too old…nope, too tight…Damn what was I thinking when I bought this? Too hot…not jazzy enough…too plain…too business like…too dark…too light…I don't know why I have not taken this to Goodwill. I'm never going to get into this again." I started a Goodwill pile in the middle of the floor. Finally, I spotted a sexy red dress I had purchased last year that still had the price tag on it. *Hallelujah!* After a quick inspection for wrinkles I decided, it was perfect. I remembered the reason I had not worn the dress was because it was loose in the places I felt it should be tight.

I kicked off my shoes, pulled my shirt over my head, and stepped out of my pants. I patted my baby roll and it jiggled. *Damn.* I unzipped the back of the dress, and stepped inside. Slowly, I eased the dress up over my thighs, but it stopped at my hips. I sucked in my stomach. The dress inched up. Determined to get it on, I walked out of the closet and stood in front of the mirror.

I paused a moment and remembered what my body looked like before my baby. I grabbed my boobs. *Big tits full of milk, and big hips. Damn.* I fought off depressing thoughts and forged on. I inhaled and pulled again. The dress moved another quarter inch. I took another deep breath and pulled.

The seams let out a melody of, 'pop…pop…pop.' I panicked and stopped breathing in the middle of a exhale. I scanned the dress line for damage. Seeing none, I tugged until the dress was over my hips. A couple of wiggles and more tugs and the dress was on. Not bad. I put my hands on my hips and posed in the mirror. Tony sat on the bed reading the instructions to his gaming system completely unconcerned with my dilemma.

"Tony, can you stop for a moment and zip me up please?"

He looked up. "Wow, you look pretty sexy for a new mom. Hold on a second. I'm going to need both hands and all my strength for this."

I glared at him. He smiled.

"I heard you in the closet grunting," he said holding back his laughter.

"Whatever. Just zip the damn dress please." I was starting to sweat. "This is ridiculous."

"Don't worry Baby, I'm going to get you into this dress one way or another; even if I have to lotion you down! Now take a deep breath." The zipper rolled up two inches. "Deeper." He struggled to get it up. "We're... almost... there. Whew... Houston, we've landed!"

I walked over to the mirror and did a 360 turn. Happy and smiling, I asked, "How do I look?"

"Beautiful! Now take it off before my parents get here." I froze in the middle of a pivot and looked at him. He was looking at me with that look in his eyes. I gave him a flimsy excuse.

"Not now, Tony. Not in front of the baby." He walked over to me.

"She's three months old, and she's asleep."

I started looking for an exit, another excuse, anything to deter him. I threw my arms up as a barrier and kept moving backwards away from his grasp. "If we start now, we're going to be late." I pleaded.

"No, we won't. I'll be fast. I promise. Come on Baby."

My back was against the dresser and I felt his hand sliding up my thigh...only he couldn't go any further because the dress was too tight.

"Damn Baby, the dress sure is tight! Turn around and I'll unzip it."

Then it hit me. When I exhaled, my stomach expanded and Tony won't be able to unzip me. "Okay Baby, unzip me." I exhaled quietly as he tried to work the zipper down.

"Baby, you have to suck it in."

Exhaling quietly I said, "I...am... sucking... it... in. Keep trying Baby." I inhaled quickly and slowly exhaled again.

"This isn't working. Where are the scissors?"

"Scissors! What are you going to do with that?"

"It's the only way to get you out of the dress."

"Quit playing." Frustrated, he stood behind me and grabbed the hem of the dress for a final pull.

'Ding-dong.' *Whew, saved by the bell.* "Coming Mother," I yelled.

Chapter 7

After 12 weeks of maternity leave, I returned to work and stayed in my office all morning. I poured over spreadsheets until my contacts dried out. I missed Rachael, and my body literally ached for her.

I took a break and swiveled my chair around and looked out of the window. I wondered how Rachael was doing and unconsciously rested my hand on top of my stomach. I felt two perfect rolls that were separated by my belt. On my way home that evening, I joined a gym and made a vow to the powers that be to get back to the size I was before I got pregnant. Over the next three months, my hard work paid off.

To celebrate a 12-pound weight loss, I put on my favorite pair of jeans with a pink tank top, and got ready to go to the mall. I grabbed the baby bag, and started packing it with diapers when the phone rang.

"Hey Ash, it's Ivy. How are you?"

Ivy was a good friend and coworker I had been working with for almost four years. Her husband, Eric, and Tony are cousins.

"I'm fine, how are you?"

"Pregnant!"

"What! Congratulations! I'm so happy for you."

"We are so excited. We have been trying for two years to get pregnant."

"I hope you have a girl so I can give you all these clothes. When is the baby due?"

"I go to the doctor next week to confirm the date, but the last time I had a period was in June, so I think I'm due around…"

I gasped. "Hold on Ivy," I dropped the phone, ran into the family room, grabbed my daily planner out my briefcase, and returned to the phone. "Ivy, you still there?"

"Yeah."

"Hold on a second; just checking something." Ivy heard me babbling and pressed her ear to the phone. I opened the planner and flipped frantically through the calendar to the month of May. Red circle. Check. Then June. No red circle. Maybe I forgot to mark it.

"Ashley! Are you okay?"

"Yes… I'm here," I whispered.

"What's wrong?" She held her breath waiting for me to respond.

"I… I missed my period last month."

Ivy hesitated and then started laughing. "That is great if we are both pregnant. We can go baby shopping, do Lamaze classes and…"

"How can I work with two babies?"

"They say it's good to have babies close together. How old is Rachael?"

"Seven months."

"Damn, that is close. Well, look on the bright side. If you have another girl, you're set."

Ivy continued to talk, but all I heard was "blah, blah, blah, and I'll call you later," before the phone went dead. I sat there staring into space when Rachael's crying jolted me back to reality. I got up, walked down to her room like a zombie, picked her up, grabbed my purse and car keys, and got in the car. Seventeen minutes later, I was in line at the drug store buying a pregnancy test kit, and gummy bears.

The ride home was a blur of stoplights and stop signs.
My first conscious thought was when I stood in front of my bathroom mirror holding Rachael on my hip as I read the instructions on the back of the kit. The instructions said the test should be taken first thing in the morning. I hesitated for a second and then ripped the box open. I sat Rachel on the floor near me, sat down on the toilet, assumed the position, and took the test.

Ten minutes later, I was staring at a solid blue "X" on a stick. *I'm pregnant.* My eyes filled with tears. I dropped my head into my hands and cried. I didn't stop until I felt a little hand touch my leg. I looked down into Rachael's big beautiful brown eyes and smiled. I called Tony and he came home early to a home filled with scented candles and soft romantic music.

"Honey, I'm home," he announced as he looked around for me. I appeared from around a corner wearing short sexy lingerie.

"Hi, Baby," I said as I approached him dangling a glass of Hennessey.

"Wow," he said, looking me up and down. "This is a nice surprise. Is Rachel asleep?"

"Yes, she is. Come sit down over here." I grabbed his hand and led him to the couch.

"Okay Baby, what's going on?"

"I'm pregnant."

He swallowed down his Hennessey, stood up, pulled me up into his arms and kissed me. "I'm going to be a daddy again! I love you." My head fell on his chest with relief. "Ash, I know we weren't planning for another baby this soon, but we'll work it out. We always find a way. I'm positioning myself to get promoted within the year. And if I am promoted, you will be able to stay home with the kids."

His words were music to my ears. "You have no idea how upset I was today."

"I could tell by the message you left something wasn't right."

I grabbed his face and kissed him. "I love you."

"You know you wouldn't be pregnant this soon if you weren't such a hot-ass." he said grabbing my butt.

"You like it hot," I said with an inviting smile.

"Yeah, I do, and now that you're pregnant, we can do it every day."

Lord help me.

On March 16, 1985 at 2:43 a.m., Michael Dean Parks arrived weighing in at a whooping 9 pounds 2 ounces.

Life is good.

Chapter 8

Seven years passed like a blur. I thought I'd never finish the 'Raising Pre-school Kids Marathon.' In retrospect, I was amazed how raising kids forced me to develop great time management skills. Over the years, I prepared the kids for day care before work, dropped them off, worked all day, picked them up, bathed and fed them, cooked dinner, did laundry, kept the house reasonably clean, and changed a thousand diapers.

Tony now came home so late from work that I was usually asleep. And lately, he hasn't been waking me up for sex—thank goodness! Between my job and the kids' after-school and Saturday sports, I rarely had time to relax. But tonight, I was going to surprise Tony.

After dinner, I tried to stay up until Tony came home, but I fell asleep and woke up with a heavy desire to pray. I laid awake trying to dismiss the urge, but it wouldn't go away. I relented to the urge and sat on the side of the bed, closed my eyes, and prayed. Two minutes later, my prayer was interrupted.

"Honey, can you stop by the cleaners and pick up my shirts today?"

I looked over my shoulder at Tony for a long hard second.

My first instinct was to say, 'No, I have enough to do after work.' But I gritted my teeth and said, "Okay."

"Thanks, Baby." He patted me on my back and went back to sleep. Prayer does work.

I got the kids ready and dropped them off at school on my way to work. The day felt longer than normal and was probably because I was not sleeping through the night. A couple of nights ago I smelled alcohol on Tony while he slept. I asked him about it, and he said he had a few beers after a hard day. I told him I wished I had the time to stop after work for a drink or two to alleviate my stress, and to let me know when he's coming home late.

After work, I picked up the kids and was almost home when I realized I forgot to stop by the cleaners. I made a left turn at the next street to turn around when out the corner of my eye I saw Tony's car parked in front of a bar. *That's odd,* I said to myself, as I made an illegal U-turn in the middle of the street. What is my husband doing in a bar? My heart started racing and I got a sick feeling in the pit of my stomach. I parked three cars behind his car.

"Kids, stay in the car and don't talk to anyone. I'll be back in five minutes. Rachael you're in charge." I faked a smile and jumped out the car.

Rachael looked at Michael and said, "Mommy runs fast."

I entered the bar expecting the worse and hoping for the best. I scanned the room in a nanosecond, and spotted Tony sitting at the bar with his arm around another woman. One second later, I was standing behind him. He was so engrossed in the conversation that he did not stop talking until he felt my seething hot breath on the back of his neck. He turned around and his eyes reflected his shock.

"Hey Ash. What are you doing here?" he said quickly pulling

his arm from around the woman.

My eyes narrowed to slits. "What are you doing here?" I asked balling my right hand into a fist by my side.

"Nothing Baby, I just stopped in to have a drink and ran into…"

"Who is this?" I said pointing at her face.

The other woman looked me up and down, took a swallow of beer and boldly said, "Baby, who is this?"

Did that heffa' just call my husband Baby? "I'm his wife! Who the hell are you?"

Tony stood up between us. My chest heaved up and down as the woman sat there stunned.

"You're married?" She stood up, grabbed her beer and stormed away.

The look on Tony's face told me all I needed to know. I drew back my right fist and fired a punch to his face, but he blocked it. *Damn police training!* I fired another punch with my left fist. He blocked the punch, grabbed my wrist, and spun me around into a restraining hold. I head-butted him.

"Ouch! Damn it Ash! Stop fighting before someone calls the police!" he said as he tightened his grip.

"Let them call so your buddies can see what a cheater you are!" A quick marital arts move freed me and I struck him, this time landing a blow to his temple. He raised his hand and rubbed his head, giving up the fight. I backed up, took one last look, and walked out.

"Ash, wait!" he yelled. "It's not what you think! Ash!"

He followed me out into the street. I ran and jumped into the car. He ran towards me and stopped when he saw the kids in the backseat.

"Mommy, there's daddy," Rachael said, waving hello. Tony smiled and waved. He dared not make a scene in front of the kids. My emotions were spiraling out of control. I was shaking and tears welled up in my eyes. I cried silently all the way home. Just like that, my marriage was over.

Chapter 9

*T*he sound of the garage door opening awakened me. Two minutes later, I heard Tony fumbling with his keys at the kitchen door. I spent the entire evening calming myself down and I swore I would wait for him to come into the bedroom before I demanded an explanation. But hearing him fumble with his keys got me angry all over again and I bolted from the bedroom to the kitchen to meet him.

I stood there and stared at the doorknob and waited. Seconds passed and I could not wait any longer. I grabbed the doorknob and yanked it open with so much force that he fell forward into the house. I looked at him with my hands on my hips.

"And where the hell have you been?" He looked surprised. I was tired, mad, angry and hungry—A really bad combination at four in the morning.

"At the bar," he said closing the door behind him. "Excuse me."

I did not, could not, and would not budge. "Who was that woman?" I asked through gritted teeth.

"What woman?" he said as he squeezed by me, making sure none of the fibers of his clothing touched me.

"You're drunk!"

He ignored me and walked out of the kitchen. I followed him into the bedroom and closed the door. He sat down on the bed, took off his shoes, laid down, and closed his eyes. I walked around the room and turned on every light and stood over him looking real crazy and waited for him to open his eyes.

"Oh no, Buddy, you're not going to sleep until you tell me who that woman was and how long you have been seeing her?" He ignored me. I jumped on the bed so hard I hoped he would fall off. "Tony," I yelled, as I dropped to my knees on the bed.

He opened his eyes, rolled out the bed, and walked out of the room. I waited for him to come back when I heard the guest bedroom door slam shut and lock. I raced down the hall, grabbed the doorknob, and tried to open it. In my blind anger I pounded the door. "Tony, open the door! Tony!" I yelled. He refused to answer. I stepped back, raised my foot and…

"Mommy, I can't sleep." I looked down the hall and saw Michael standing in the hallway rubbing his eyes.

Damn. I lowered my leg and said loud enough for Tony to hear, "This isn't over."

I walked over to Michael, picked him up, and carried him into his room. After Michael fell asleep, I returned to my bedroom and fell into the bed. All I could think about was my life as a wife was over. And the horrific thing about the whole situation was, I still loved him. *Oh Lord, what am I going to do?*

Chapter 10

I woke up and Tony was gone. Anger started to consume me again before I realized he worked on Saturdays. My head was throbbing and I walked into the bathroom for Aspirin. I stood in front of the mirror and wondered who the person was looking back. The sparkle in my eyes was replaced with sadness. I saw a couple of gray strands peeping through my wild hair... and a pimple. I opened the medicine cabinet, shook two Aspirin out of the bottle, and washed them down with water.

"Mom," Rachael said, "Tell Michael to stop changing the channel."

I gave her 'the look.' Her eyes got real big, and she ran out of the bathroom. I took a deep breath and went through my day on autopilot. I called my parents and asked if the kids could spend the night to give me a break. They agreed and stopped by to pick them up. An hour later, I heard the garage door open. I shifted my position on the sofa from lying down to sitting, turned the television down, and waited. Tony entered the house, threw his keys on the counter, and headed to the bedroom.

I shouted, "Tony!" To my surprise he stopped. I softened my tone to a "Come here… please." He took a moment to assess my demeanor. When he felt it was safe, he walked over and sat down at the other end of the couch.

"What's going on Tony? And please, don't act like you don't know what I'm talking about."

He looked down. "I'm working undercover on a drug case, Ash."

You're lying! I screamed on the inside. But on the outside, I remained cool. "I see. That's why she called you Baby, right?"

"That wasn't the first time I've seen her," Tony said, looking straight into my eyes. "I have been working on this case for months. I can't tell you any more than that, Ash. I know it looked bad seeing me in the bar. I would never cheat on you, or do anything to break our family up. I love you too much for that."

I looked for a twitch or any subtle body movement that would indicate he was lying, but nothing set off my alarm. Maybe he was telling the truth. My wall of anger began to slowly crumble.

"Prove it. Prove this is a case and not an affair."

He moved over and attempted to put his arm over my shoulder but I stopped him. "I'm not there yet," I said, gently moving his arm away. "I want proof, and I want it now."

"I can't get it now. I'll get it later."

My feet moved before he could finish his sentence. I got off the couch, walked in the bedroom, closed the door, and locked it.

Chapter 11

Monday afternoon, I walked into a local bank during my lunch hour and opened another savings account. I returned to work and to keep my mind off of Tony, I buried myself in work, and pretended to everyone around me that my life was normal. After work, I picked up the kids and stopped by a fast food restaurant to pick up dinner. Twenty minutes later, we were in the kitchen eating when the garage door opened. Tony walked in. Instead of speaking, I ignored him.

"Daddy!" the kids yelled and raced to jump into his arms. He swooped them up in his arms and kissed them on their foreheads. The thought of breaking them up hurt my heart.

"Hi Ash," he said with a hint of remorse.

"Hi. You got proof yet?"

"Still working on it. What's for dinner?"

"Peanut butter and jelly," I said, wanting to laugh at the surprised look on his face. The nerve of him to think I'm going to cook for him. "No proof, no dinner."

I opened the pantry door, grabbed the Yellow Pages, and headed to the bedroom. I flopped on the bed and thumbed through pages of advertisements for divorce attorneys. A few minutes later, Tony walked in and sat down next to me. "What do you want?" I asked dryly.

"You were right," he said.

I slammed the book shut. "Right about what?"

"The woman in the bar."

I snapped and the street brawler in me came out. I swung wildly at him before he was able to restrain me face down on the bed with my arms behind me.

"Get off me you lying, cheating piece of shit, before I scream!"

"You won't scream because you don't want to scare the kids." He was right.

"Get off me!" I shouted as I wiggled one arm free. He grabbed it and restrained me again.

"If you move again, I'm going to handcuff you!" he threatened.

"What!"

"You know I can have you arrested for assault, and I have the scratches to prove it!"

"If you throw me in jail, I guarantee you this, when I get out you will wish you had never met me."

"Then calm down and listen. Please, Ash, I'm tired of fighting."

I struggled to free my arms but he pressed his body weight down and made it impossible for me to move. Against my will, I relented. "Okay, I'll stop only if you release my arms!"

"You promise? I know how you are." He eased the pressure off my arms just enough for me to get some relief, but not enough for me to get free. He knew me well. "Ash... I'm sorry. I was wrong."

"Sorry for what?"

"Everything I put you through."

"Why Tony? Why did you cheat on me?" I wiped my tears on

the bed.

"I don't know. Attention. You always complain about how tired you are."

"I'm tired because you don't help me do anything. Did you…" I asked but really didn't want to know.

"No…I didn't."

I wanted to believe him even if he was lying. My heart could not handle that truth.

"Did you want to?"

"I'd be lying if I said it didn't cross my mind. I didn't do it because of our vows. I know you want to leave me and I don't blame you. Don't leave Ash. I'll do anything to keep us together."

"Anything?"

"Anything," he said with a ray of hope.

"Find me a good attorney."

"How about a marriage counselor?"

"I don't need counseling. You need counseling. You're the one who cheated."

"All I'm asking for is a second chance. I know I messed up and…"

"I'll think about it."

"Mom!" Rachael yelled. "Grandma is on the phone!"

"Tell Grandma to hold on, I'll be right there."

Tony released me. I glared at him with disdain in my eyes. He reached to hug me and I jerked away. Clearing my voice, I picked up the phone, "Hi, Mom."

Chapter 12

*T*hree months passed and I finally agreed to accompany Tony to a counseling session. On my way, I got stuck in traffic and arrived late. Tony looked relieved when I walked in.

"Good afternoon. How may I help you?" the receptionist asked.

"Hi, my name is Ashley Parks, and I'm here to see Dr. Dukes."

"Hi, Ms. Parks, may I see a photo ID and a copy of your insurance card, please?"

I showed her my license, and informed her that Mr. Parks was paying for the visit.

"Thank you," she said, and handed me a clipboard. "Please fill out this form, the questionnaire on the back, and sign here. When you are finished give the questionnaire to Dr. Dukes."

I sat near Tony, but intentionally left an empty seat between us. Five minutes later, a door opened and a tall handsome African-American man entered wearing a navy-blue tailored suit with a crisp white shirt.

"Mr. and Mrs. Parks?" We nodded. "Good afternoon, I'm Dr. Dukes. No pun intended." He laughed at his own joke. Tony and I exchanged an 'oh, boy,' look. The doctor shook Tony's hand, and

I said hello.

We followed Dr. Dukes down a long hallway lined with beautiful artwork. His office was large enough to accommodate a custom-made mahogany floor-to-ceiling bookcase, matching desk, sofa, and two wingback chairs. I admired his trophy wall, which was full of college degrees, awards, and news articles about his business. *Impressive.*

He gestured for us to sit in the wingback chairs in front of his desk. He sat down at his desk and put on his glasses. After a quick review of our paperwork, he looked over the rim of his glasses and asked, "Mr. and Mrs. Parks, why did you come see me today?"

Tony looked over at me and I kept my eyes locked on the therapist. He took a deep breath, but before he could answer I blurted out, "My husband cheated on me. And since it's a crime to commit murder, I figured I'd come here instead."

Tony coughed, and the therapist cleared his throat. "Well, I'm glad you came in today," he said as he picked up his pen and made a note. "Is that true Mr. Parks?"

Tony sat up straight and clasped his hands together. "Dr. Dukes, we have two children, and I want to keep my family together."

"He asked you if that was true?" I said calmly.

"Yeah, sort of." He dropped his head.

"I see."

"Mrs. Parks, what do you want to do?"

"I want him to tell me the truth. I want to know why and how long the affair has been going on. I thought about kicking him out, but the kids love him so much it would hurt them more than it would hurt me." My voice cracked, and I stopped talking.

"Mrs. Parks, I know you are hurting, and you have every right to feel the way you do. Your husband betrayed your trust, and now it appears he wants to do everything he can to keep the marriage together. My question for you is, do you want to stay married to Tony?"

I sat there mute for a full minute. "Part of me does because we have been married eight years, and I don't want to hurt the kids. If I didn't have kids, we'd be spending this money on an attorney."

"I understand. The first thing we need to do is to focus on getting the trust back in the marriage. That means Tony, if you have to call her every hour on the hour, you call her."

I smiled. *Get him!*

"Dr. Parks, I do that now," Tony said in his defense. I call five times a day and she still won't let it go. Every chance she gets, she brings it up. I don't know what else to do."

I sat up straight and pointed at Tony. "If you called me ten times a day and said you are at work, how do I know you're not lying?"

"Ash, how can I prove to you I'm not lying?"

"You lied about the affair. Why should I believe you now!"

Frustrated, Tony shook his head. "I don't know what else I can do to convince you I won't cheat again. This is why I'm here. I love you and don't want to lose you. I'm sorry Ash. I'm sorry!" He looked up at the ceiling and closed his eyes.

"How long?" I asked. Dr. Dukes kept writing. "How long!"

He refused to answer. I looked at Dr. Dukes. "He won't tell me how long he cheated on me. Just, 'I'm sorry.' And that's a problem."

"Tony is there a specific reason why you won't answer your wife?"

"What difference does it make? I'm trying to keep us together, not bring up stuff to keep us apart."

"Tony what are you willing to do to keep your marriage together?"

"Anything."

"Then answer the question."

Tony shifted his position in his chair and wrung his hands. "Six months," he mumbled. I gripped the bottom of my chair and stopped myself from propelling out of my seat and attacking Tony.

"Ashley, I can see this is very painful for you. Tell me how you feel right now."

"I'm so angry right now I can't think. I don't want to see his face around the house again. The last six months of my marriage has been a lie. Here I am working, cooking, cleaning, raising his children, and every time he told me he loved me, it was a lie. A LIE! I hate you Tony!"

The therapist handed me a box of tissues, and Tony got up and kneeled down by my side.

"Baby, I am so sorry. I'm sorry." He whispered as he tried desperately to console me. Numb with pain, he held me while I sobbed uncontrollably. After what seemed like an hour, I stopped, and slowly regained my composure.

"Are you feeling better Mrs. Parks?" I looked at the therapist and nodded yes, even though I didn't. I laid my head on Tony's shoulder, and for the first time in months felt a connection.

"If you want to stay married, both of you are going to have to work at it. Tony, moving forward, when Ashley vents, let her. Her anger will slowly decline over time. You have to be patient to make this work." He glanced at the clock. "Tony, you are moving in the right direction. Continue to call her every day. We will talk more about this next week. Thank you for coming in. I look forward to seeing you soon."

Chapter 13

*A*fter Tony dropped the 'six-month-affair bombshell' at the first session, I did not return to therapy. My heart was not in the marriage any more but I pretended I was happy around the kids. I did not force Tony to leave because of the kids, and that turned out to be a good decision.

He continued to see the therapist, and over time, I did notice a positive change in his behavior. He surprised me with gifts, he cut back on his overtime, and he spent more time with the family. He was doing everything he could to keep us together, and it was working. A year passed, and the affair had finally moved from a daily thought to an afterthought. I started to fall back in love. Tony was thoughtful, compassionate, generous, and loving. I was cautiously happy again.

This weekend, we will celebrate our ninth anniversary. I made arrangements for my parents to watch the kids. I wondered what Tony would buy me this time. My jewelry box was getting full. I decided to surprise him and cook his favorite meal, Lasagna. I had enough time to have it ready before he arrived home. I opened the refrigerator, removed all the necessary ingredients, and started cooking when the phone rang.

"Hello?…Hello?" The line went dead. *Hmm… probably a wrong number.*

The phone rang again. This time I answered with an attitude. "Hello!" Still, no answer, but I could tell someone was there. "Who is this?" No answer. I slammed the phone down. Being married to a cop, when someone calls and hangs up, it made me uneasy.

Around seven o'clock, I grew tired of waiting and called the kids to the table for dinner. I started to worry and called Tony. No answer. My emotions spiked from worry to anger. The kids finished eating and I sent them to bed before their normal bedtime. They protested but quickly changed their mind when I gave them 'the look'.

Six hours later, the garage door opened waking me out of a sleep I had not planned. I looked at the alarm clock. Twice. It was 2:10 a.m.! When the garage door closed I jumped out the bed, ran into the kitchen and waited in front of the door. I heard him fumbling with his keys. Déjà vu. I waited. He opened the door and stumbled in.

"Hey Baby, what you doing up this late?" He was drunk.

I wondered how the hell he drove home in his condition. "I'm up because you were suppose to be home six hours ago. Where were you?" I asked in a restrained tone.

"I was out with the guys," he said as he opened the fridge and grabbed a beer.

"Why didn't you call?"

Tony twisted the cap off the beer and took a swig. "I didn't call, because I didn't feel like arguing."

"In other words, you just didn't give a damn?"

"See, what I mean? Give me a kiss."

He leaned into me and I got a whiff of perfume. I leaned back and frowned. He took his beer into the living room and plopped down on the couch. Without saying a word, I stormed out the kitchen and locked myself in the bedroom. *This time Tony, I am not going to be in the dark.* I waited for him pass out on the couch and listened intently for 'the signal'. The first snore. Five minutes later, I heard him snoring. I walked into the living room and stood over him.

"Tony!" I said loudly. He continued to snore. I checked his shirt pocket and found a couple of meaningless receipts. I slid my hand carefully down his front pocket and felt a bunch of change. My heart beat faster as I gently rolled him over and tried to ease his wallet out of his back pocket. He started mumbling. Scared that I might wake him I gave up. Frustrated, I sat down and stared at the TV. A commercial came on advertising a new car. At that instant, I realized I overlooked his car. I jumped off the couch and ran into the garage.

I walked over to his car, opened the passenger door, sat down, and looked for evidence. I turned the inside light on and felt around the side of the seat, under the seat, and looked inside the armrest. *Nothing. Shit!* I opened the glove compartment. *Nothing!* Everything looked normal. I opened the door to get out and before I stood up, I paused and flipped the lid on the ashtray open. *Bingo.* I held the remains of a cigarette butt with red lipstick on it up to the light.

I do not remember turning off the car light, closing the car door, or passing through the kitchen. All I remember is standing over Tony with the cigarette butt, yelling at the top of my lungs. I yelled so loudly that I woke up the kids, the dog next door started barking, and the neighbors' outside motion light came on. Everyone woke up, but Tony.

One year later, on November 2, 1992 at the pound of the gavel, the judge announced our divorce.

The recycling process has begun.

Three Phases to
RECYCLING
HUSBANDS

Phase One:
Healing

You are divorced. For many of you this may be an emotionally painful time, and for others, the party is just beginning. To successfully recycle husbands, the goal is to let go of the past and any resentment you may have in order to move forward within a timely manner. If you are feeling bitter, remorseful, and want to ban your ex-husband to hell, the healing process will help you move pass those emotions.

Some of the common symptoms you may experience are the following: sleep deprivation, depression, mood swings, crying spells, sweet cravings, weight gain or weight loss, compulsive shopping, regret, and a desire to use prescription drugs and/or alcohol.

To help you migrate through those symptoms, you will need to enlist a friend to help you navigate down the path to healing. Focus on recruiting a friend who has a positive attitude and is not currently experiencing any major drama. Other endearing qualities to look for are:

Patience—Your friend should not mind being contacted any hour of the day or night to offer moral support.

Empathy Skills—They should understand the pain and anger you may be experiencing, and be able to reserve criticism. If you drink occasionally, it would be nice to have a friend to occasionally stop by announced or unannounced with dinner and a bottle of wine. Your friend should be understanding and generous with offerings of mental and spiritual support.

If you are not sleeping through the night, work on a plan that will systematically eliminate the issues going on in your life (within your control) that cause stress. How? Focus on eliminating one issue at a time and not all at once. Write down everything that is causing the stress. Then go over your list and prioritize from the least stressful to the most stressful. Start with the least stressful issue and make a plan to eliminate it and stick to the plan.

The feeling of depression before, during, and after a divorce is common for many. Others may experience a sense of relief and joy and will skip through the Healing Phase and dive right into the 'Dating Phase'.

Crying releases stress. If you are crying a lot, put yourself on a crying schedule. Cry the first week ten minutes in the morning, and ten minutes in the evening. The second week, cry five minutes in the morning, and five minutes in the evening. Continue to decrease your crying time until you have stopped. Most of you may be on this schedule only two days.

After a divorce, some of you may occasionally schedule a secret rendezvous with the ex-husband in the wee hours of the morning for some physical attention. If so, start weaning yourself off of your ex-husband until the desire is gone. Replacing him with another person is not recommended.

Your salt and sugar cravings may surge during this time. If you have noticed your consumption of these products has increased dramatically, take control, NOW! Replace cakes, donuts, potato chips, cookies, hamburgers, French fries, candy, ice cream, and soda with healthy snacks.

Shop until you drop—if it is within your budget. It is very hard to be depressed when you are buying yourself a new outfit or a new pair of shoes. If you are on a budget, set up a plan to pay off debt (one credit card at a time over 12 months) and attempt to stick to it. If you have a lot of debt, seek professional counseling.

Drugs, alcohol, and prescription medication may impair your judgment and is not recommended for long-term use.

Create a durable, and flexible 'Action Plan' to become mentally, physically, and financially stronger within 12 months. Write down the plan and include three or more reasonable goals and details explaining how you plan to accomplish it.

For example, if you want a better paying job and the job requires more skills, create a plan to take an online class. If you want to save money, set up automatic deposits to a savings account. If you need help creating a plan, consult a Life Coach, a friend, minister, family member, or therapist for assistance. As you grow stronger and several months have passed, you may notice a few subtle changes.

a) You wake up in the morning and your ex-husband is NOT the first thought that enters your mind. You are making progress.

b) The desire to call your ex-husband at night becomes an after thought.

c) You are sleeping in the middle of the bed and not on 'your' side.

d) You have limited your communication with those individuals who kept you in the drama loop.

e) You have removed your wedding band.

f) You can say your ex-husband's name without using profanity.

g) You understand the pain of loneliness was temporary.

h) When people ask you, "Why did you get divorced?" you can smile and politely respond, "We both made mistakes and decided to move on." And smile.

Congratulations! You are now familiar with the common symptoms you may experience after a divorce. You have recruited a friend to help you move forward over the next year, you have created a flexible and durable 'Action Plan' to become mentally, emotionally, and financially stronger. Now it is time to move to Phase Two: Fitness.

Phase Two:
Fitness

Exercise is highly recommended when you are recycling husbands. Check with your physician before starting an exercise plan. During this phase, your focus will be on increasing your physical activity through various activities such as: walking, swimming, cycling, or running. Integrating a fitness routine into your weekly schedule will help prepare your body for Phase Three: Dating. If you are already in shape, keep up the good work.

This Phase is also known as the 'feel good phase'. The goal is to not only feel healthy, but also look healthy. Take a moment to decide if you want to work out in the morning, afternoon, or evening. Next, determine what type of activity you want to do.

Here are some suggestions to help you get started:
*Join a gym
*Take a yoga class or spin class
*Learn martial arts
*Swim, jog, rock climb, water or snow ski
*Belly dance
*Take a Zumba class
*Walk around the mall
*Run on a treadmill
*Walk around the block on your lunch hour

If you cannot exercise thirty minutes a day, attempt to exercise 5-10 minutes a day or every other day and gradually increase the amount of time you exercise every week. Within 30 days, you will notice your stamina will have increased, and you may notice a slight weight loss. Be patient with the results.

If you struggle with weight issues, there are a variety of weight loss programs available that can help you lose the weight. Most fitness centers offer a personal trainer service. Take advantage of those services.

Plan to exercise a minimum of 90 days. The benefit is that your energy level will increase, and you will start to look and feel better. Set a goal to obtain and/or maintain a body size that is in proportion to your height and stick to it. If possible, continue exercising after you have met your goals. If you stop exercising for a while, attempt to resume the activity at a later time. Make a commitment to embrace exercise as a lifetime commitment. You can do this. Take charge of your life and funnel some of that same passion, and energy into taking charge of your fitness.

Phase Three:
Dating

Dating, whether it is done in person or over the Internet is a time consuming process designed to help you select a mate. A majority of the male population are visual creatures. They see, they like, they conquer- a primal male instinct for most of them.

The females' primal instinct is to select the strongest mate after they compete for her affection (Animal Kingdom 101). However, in the real world there are some men and women who have a terrific personality, steady income, are moderately attractive, who want a mate but have been rejected so often that they have exiled themselves to a life of dating. Your goal is to find a husband, not a lifetime boyfriend.

Let's get started with two easy rules.

Rule #1: A simple and easy way to get someone's attention is to smile. Do not under estimate the power of a smile. It is a formidable asset to use to attract a mate.

Rule #2: Be Happy. When you are happy, you create a positive field of energy around you. Positive energy attracts people. Before you dive into the dating world, take a moment and think about the type of man you want to attract. Do you want a blue-collar worker, a white-collar worker, or a no-collar worker?

Does he have strong personality traits and qualities that will hold up well over time? Is he kind and compassionate? Does he have manners? Is he spiritual? Does he have a good relationship with his mother/sister/grandmother/aunt? Is he happy?

Knowing what traits you would like to see in a man will

help you screen out the wrong candidates faster. There are no perfect men, and there are no perfect women, so set reasonable expectations.

How to increase your dating opportunities:
1) Become a full time or part-time college student. Enroll in classes where the industry is known to be male dominated (auto mechanics, computer technology, criminal justice, carpentry, plumbing and heating, aviation, anthropology, communications, physics, political science, military science, and any engineering discipline, just to name a few).

2) Introduce yourself to a single co-worker. If you are not comfortable introducing yourself, have another co-worker introduce you.

3) Physical fitness centers are very popular. Visit a gym during peak hours, and make a mental note of the ratio of men to women. Join a gym that appears to have a good balanced ratio.

4) Attend outdoor concerts with friends. Outdoor concerts offer a relaxed atmosphere for meeting people.

5) Join an online dating site. Keep in mind that approximately 80% of the profile information may be inflated. Proceed with caution, always meet in a public space, and let your friends know who you are meeting, and where. Use an alternate phone number such as Google voice for extra security.

6) Get involved with charity walks, marathons, and cycling events.

7) Attend major sporting events, or watch a major sporting event at a sports bar with a female friend.

8) Take your dog to the park for an extended walk. Wear your best jogging outfit with a little make-up, and fashionable jogging shoes. If you see someone interesting, start a brief conversation about dogs.

9) Invite your 'Man-Magnet' girlfriend to go out with you. Explain the details of the plan and go from there.

10) Attend your high school reunion.

11) Join a social media site to locate old friends.

12) Get involved with organizations that may offer activities and events for single members.

13) Ask a friend or co-worker to introduce you to one of their single and available family member or friends.

14) Explore job transfer opportunities to a larger town or city.

15) Take firearm or bow lessons.

Now that you have a mate in mind, the discovery questions below are designed to help you with the screening process. Focus on getting answers to the questions that are applicable to your situation. Remember, you are looking for a husband, not a boyfriend.

1)   Is he married?
2)   Is he employed?
3)   Does he believe in a higher spiritual power?
4)   What religion, if any, does he believe in?
5)   Does he live within his means?
6)   What is his credit score?
7)   Does he get angry quickly?
8)   Does he smoke?

9)   Does he drink and/or gamble responsibly or at all?

10) Is he addicted to porn?

11) What hereditary diseases exist in his family?

12) Have you caught him in a lie?

13) Will you like your in-laws?

14) Does he make you laugh?

15) Is he generous or selfish?

16) Has anyone referred to him as crazy (not the funny type of crazy; the call 911 crazy)?

17) Is he overly jealous?

18) If you call him at 7 a.m. or 11:30 p.m., does the phone go to voicemail?

19) How many kids is he supporting—or not supporting?

20) Will your kids like him?

21) Does he have a relationship with his kids, or does he just pay child support?

22) What type of relationship does he have with the mother(s) of his children?

23) Will he allow you to pursue your dreams or will you be helping him achieve his dreams?

Now that the screening process is over and you have a couple of solid candidates and are struggling with your decision on which ones to eliminate, I can help you with that. Most men are expecting to have sex after a couple of dates. If you really like the guy, not having sex with him will reveal more of his true character.

For example, if you have been dating for about a month and he comes on to you and you tell him "No, I want to get to know you better," and he smiles and says "'Okay," and you don't hear from him the rest of the week, he was not the one for you.

If you have been dating two months and you tell him "No, I'm not comfortable with that yet," and he continues to call you, he is demonstrating that he values and respects your decision to wait. He may also be waiting to see how long it takes you to cave in, and is just playing along because he can pay 'Miss Easy' for a visit while he waits. If that is the case, he is not the one for you. Men love a challenge and for most of them the thrill is in the chase.

Hold your ground and MAKE HIM WAIT! How long? Four months is the minimum. It is important to become familiar with his common and uncommon behaviors now rather than later. If he is willing to wait and does not cheat during that time, I would say you are off to a very good start. Make SEX the bonus in the relationship, not the qualifier.

Now that Ashley has completed the Healing and Fitness phases, she is ready to start dating.

RECYCLING HUSBANDS
Part Two

Chapter 14

Ashley, now 35 and ready to start dating, called her friend Laurie for moral support. Laurie had been married to Don for twelve years, and had three sons. Don, a former NFL player played in the league for six years after he graduated from the University of Maryland. His career ended after a serious knee injury. He worked as an assistant football coach at his alma mater. Laurie, was a full-time mom and loved home schooling her children.

"Hey Laurie. What's going on?" I asked as I watched the tourists outside my office window walk around the Baltimore Harbor.

"Nothing. Just preparing lunch for the boys. How are you?"

"Good and thinking about dating again."

"You met someone?"

"Not really. But I did notice this nice looking guy in the cafeteria this morning.

"Well, at least you know he's employed."

"Yeah, you're right."

"Ash, Don has a friend that has been divorced for a couple of years named Neal. I think you might like him."

"Neal, hmmm… I like that name. Tell me more."

"He is about six feet tall, medium build, 190 pounds, mustache, sandy brown complexion, bald, and has a beautiful smile."

"Why is he divorced?"

"I don't know all the details. All I know is he has custody of his girls."

"Why do you want me to meet him?"

"Because Neal stopped by last Saturday with his daughters and I overhead him telling Don that he is ready to settle down, but he can't find a woman that is not interested in his money."

"Money? How many kids does he have?"

"Two. And I believe he is still living in Columbia, Maryland. His father owns a national moving truck company, and he is the only heir to the throne."

"Does he work for his father?"

"No, he works for a pharmaceutical company. He's in sales and he travels a lot."

"If he travels a lot, he probably spends a lot of time away from home. That might not work for me."

"Next weekend I'm having a barbecue. Plan to come; I know you are not doing anything. I will tell Don to invite Neal and another friend of his, named Connor."

"Who's Connor?"

"He is another close friend of Don's I think you will like. They grew up together. He joined the Air Force after high school and made a career out of it. He has lived all over the world and is stationed at Andrews Air Force Base. He lives a few miles away in Upper Marlboro."

"What does he do in the Air Force?"

"He's a pilot, and looks really good in uniform. Really good!"

"Is he divorced?

"Yup. Was married for a short period of time. I'll ask Don what happened. Well, I have to go feed these kids. I'll call you later."

Chapter 15

Saturday morning, the phone rings.

"Ash, wake up, and get over here and help me cook," Laurie demanded before I could even say hello.

"What time is it?"

"Eight o'clock."

"Ughh…my head is killing me. I'm not going to make it," I said whispering into the phone.

"Girl, take two Motrin. You're not backing out now. I will see you in a couple of hours. Oh, and wear something cute and sexy."

***

Four hours later I knocked on Laurie's door.

"Ash! I was just about to call you. Come on in," Laurie said. She hugged me as if she had not seen me in years. I looked around the room and recognized most of the couples she had invited; many of them I had not seen since Tony and I divorced. As I walked through the room everyone complimented me on how good I looked. I felt like a million dollars.

"Ash…over here," Laurie said as she waved me her way.

"Everybody, out please! Thank you." Laurie led me into the

kitchen where she wanted to have a private conversation.

"Why are you wearing slacks and a business shirt? You look like you just left the office!"

"I didn't have anything else to wear," I said to my defense. Laurie started unbuttoning my shirt from the neck.

"What are you doing?" I slapped her hands away.

"Stop it! How do you expect to attract a man buttoned up to the neck like Saint Theresa?"

"I don't need to show my cleavage to get a man's attention." I started buttoning my shirt.

"Yes, you do! Now stop being difficult." Laurie slapped my hand again.

"No!" I put my hands over my buttons.

Laurie stepped back and threw her hands on her hips. "Look, I'm not asking you to strip. Just unbutton one little button!"

I saw she was determined to get her way, so I relented. "I'll do it." I unbuttoned one button, but Laurie didn't budge. I undid another and my breasts popped out like they were trying to escape my bra.

Laurie gave a sigh of relief. "Pulling nails out of wood would be easier."

I looked down at my cleavage and adjusted my shirt to minimize my exposure.

"Don't bother, you're too big." She reached in her pocket and handed me a compact mirror, eyeliner, and lip-gloss. "Put this on."

She then led me over to the French doors that led to the backyard and directed my attention to the pool. "Look over there. See that group of guys. That one is Neal and the other one is Connor."

"Which one is Neal?"

"Neal is the one wearing a navy blue polo shirt and jeans."

"Hmm… not bad. And Connor?"

"The one on Neal's right, wearing khaki shorts and a peach shirt."

"He's nice looking too," I applied another coat of lip-gloss.

Laurie walked over to the kitchen counter and picked up a bowl of potato salad. "Take this and follow me."

I put my shades on, grabbed the bowl, and followed her outside onto a large teak wooden deck. I sat the potato salad between the Caesar salad and the coleslaw. It felt awkward being around my married friends without Tony. I followed Laurie over to a group of friends and started talking.

I could see Neal out of the corner of my eye, looking in my direction. I repositioned my stance to keep him in my peripheral vision as I continued my conversation, but I could not stop myself from glancing at him and it appeared he was having the same issue. Eventually, I smiled at him and he waved back.

Moments later, he ended his conversation and made his way toward me. I panicked a little and turned around and bumped into a guy wearing khaki shorts and a peach shirt.

"Oops…I'm sorry." I said as I backed up. "I did not see you."

"No, problem. You didn't damage anything. My name is Connor."

"I'm Ashley. It's nice to meet you. Sorry about spilling your beer. Can I buy you another one?" He laughed. "It's nice chatting with you, Connor."

"Yes and hopefully, I will see you later."

I smiled and walked over to Laurie.

"Laurie, I just bumped into Connor."

"And?"

"And you were right! He is FINE! I can't believe he doesn't have a girlfriend."

"What did he say?"

"I bumped into him and…"

"Hey Laurie, Don is over there taking credit for your barbecue sauce, you better straighten him out," said Neal as he approached us.

"Oh no he isn't! I'll be back." Laurie marched right over to Don.

"Hi, I'm Neal. And you are…"

"Ashley, and it's nice to meet you." I smiled.

"Are you enjoying yourself?"

"Yes, I am. It's nice seeing my old friends again."

"You don't live around here?"

"No, I do. I lost touch with most of my married friends after I got divorced."

"I understand. The same thing happened to me."

"How long have you been divorced?"

"Three years. And you?"

"A little over a year."

The rest of the afternoon Neal and I talked about sports, kids, and single parenting and realized we had a lot in common. He had to leave the party early, but we exchanged numbers and promised to keep in touch. When the other guests started to leave, I stayed and helped Laurie clean up.

"Laurie you were right?" I said smiling.

"About what?"

"About Neal. We did hit it off."

"I noticed. What about Connor?"

"He's nice looking and seems nice. I really didn't get a chance to talk to him."

"Good, because Connor wants you to call him. He asked me to give you this."

Laurie handed me his number. I left the party feeling like a queen.

Chapter 16

I called Connor the next day, and we met for lunch at my favorite seafood restaurant. Secretly, I had hoped I would run into Tony so he could see how great I looked without him. We talked so long that our lunch date almost turned into a dinner date. We agreed to meet again, and over the next several weeks we continued to date.

Connor was worldly, sensitive, intelligent, and grew up in a military family. He was divorced with no kids, and had a high-level security clearance that required him to keep secrets and travel abroad. While I could see him as an excellent provider, I could not see myself being home alone most of the time, and knowing that he was keeping secrets made me a little uncomfortable.

Neal was funny, intelligent, and family oriented. He was a regional manager for a major pharmaceutical company, and had full custody of his daughters. We talked a couple of times a week and met for lunch a few times when he was in my area. Dating two guys at the same time was starting to eat into my 'me' time. I had to let one go.

Connor called me that evening and said he was leaving the

country for an assignment and did not know when he would be back. At the end of our conversation, we agreed we could only be friends. With Connor out of the picture, I focused more of my leisure time around Neal. One evening, after a movie date with Neal, I asked him why he was divorced? A solemn look came across his face.

"I was wondering when you were going to ask me that," he said keeping his eyes on the road as he drove. "I got divorced because my wife left me for another man, and moved to another state. After she left, I found out she had been having an affair for years with a coworker."

I thought about Tony's affair and sighed. "How did the girls take it?"

"The girls cried for days. You cannot imagine the heartache and anger I experienced," he said. I thought, *Oh, yes I can.*

We stopped at the light and he turned to me, and looked into my eyes. "My oldest daughter, Janice, suffered in silence. She didn't talk to anyone for weeks. My youngest daughter, Joyce, cried herself to sleep in my arms every night for two weeks. How do you comfort your baby when she clings to you in tears and says, 'I want my Mommy?' What kind of mother abandons her kids?" he said in a whisper, as if he were talking to himself.

"I'm sorry Neal. I didn't mean to dredge up a painful memory."

"I know. I was going to tell you sooner or later anyway. What is crazier is, I wanted her back so my daughters could stop hurting. So, I searched for her and tried to find out where she was. In retrospect, I'm glad I didn't find her. Counseling helped us get through it. I have forgiven Jackie, and I hope one day my daughters will be able to do the same."

He pulled into my driveway and turned off the engine. He said he was over it, but I could still see the pain in his eyes. I recognized the look. I kissed Neal good night, got out of the car, and made a mental note to never ask about Jackie again.

Neal lowered his window and yelled, "I love you!"

I turned around, smiled, and yelled, "I love you more!"

***

We continued to date over the next six months. The kids knew about Neal, but never met him. Neal said his girls were anxious to meet me, and after what we felt was a generous period of time for us to get to know one another, we decided to get our kids together. We talked about how we felt about marriage and were both on the same page, however, if the kids do not like Neal, and his daughters do not like me, the relationship was doomed to become a friendship with an expiration date.

Neal, Janice, and Joyce met us at a popular barbecue restaurant in downtown Baltimore. Rachael and Janice were 12 years old, Michael was 11, and Joyce was 10. At first they all played the shy role, but by the time they finished dessert you would have thought they were best friends—everyone except Michael. By him being the only boy, he just watched and listened.

After dating for more than a year, Neal asked me to marry him, and I joyfully accepted. Six months later, I was Mrs. Neal West. We honeymooned in Maui for a week without the kids. Several months later, we sold our homes and bought a new five-bedroom home in Columbia, Maryland. The kids were getting along well and lived close enough to their old friends to still get together with them over the weekends.

Life was good.

Chapter 17

*J*ust when I started to dispel those nightmare stories about blended families, Janice and Joyce started to complain to Neal that he was not spending enough time with them. Rachael started to complain that I was spending more time with Janice and Joyce than her. And Michael started to complain about not spending time with Tony.

To keep the peace, I came up with a solution. We designated one day a week as a Fun day. Neal would spend that day with his daughters, and I would spend the day with Rachael and Michael. Three months passed by without any drama.

One morning while making coffee, Rachael walked in and told me that Janice was in love with Chase, the 15-year-old boy next door. I informed Neal, and he became concerned about Janice seeing the boy during the day while we were at work. He asked me to talk to Janice about sex.

The next evening, I sat down with all the girls and asked them what they knew about sex. Janice threw her hand in the air with no shame, and confessed to know everything. To top it off, she started sharing it all and it took all of my facial muscle strength to stop my mouth from dropping open.

"In the sex education class, they showed us the different condom sizes; you can get them lubricated; they have different flavors and..."

"Thank you Janice for that information," I interrupted.

"I know about sex too," Joyce said proudly.

"I'm sure you do, and I'm glad all of you do know something about sex, but did you know you shouldn't have sex until you are married."

"I don't want to wait. Did you wait until you were married?" asked Janice.

The phone rang. *Thank God!* I cleared my throat. "Yes, I did wait until I was married, and you're going to wait too!"

"Honey, it's for you. Memorial Hospital?" said Neal.

I walked over to him and took the phone out of his hand. "Hello Mrs. Parks, my name is Tanya, and I am an emergency nurse at Memorial Hospital in Ellicott City. We admitted your husband, Tony Parks into the hospital and we need you to come to the hospital as soon as possible."

"What happened?"

"He was shot and we are working on him now. He's in the emergency room and he requested we contact you."

Tears stung my eyes. "Tony! Is he going to be okay?"

"He's being prepped for surgery. I don't know the extent of his wounds."

Rachael overheard me say Tony's name, and came over and stood by me. I choked back the tears.

"Ok, I'll be right there."

"Enter the hospital through the Emergency Room. It will be easier to find him," the nurse said.

"Mom, is Dad okay?" Rachael asked with the most frightened look on her face.

"Right now, I don't know."

Neal grabbed his car keys, and in a calm voice, told the kids we would be back as soon as we could. On the way to the hospital, my mind played out all kinds of 'what if' scenarios. What if he dies before I get there? What if he's paralyzed? What if he has a brain injury? I even thought about the first time we met on campus, our honeymoon, our kids, and how much we once loved each other. I went through a wave of emotions in thirty seconds. My eyes welled up with tears.

I looked out of the passenger side window and tried to rapidly blink the tears away. I did not want Neal to see me crying over Tony.

"How did they know to call you?" he asked, breaking the silence, which brought me back to reality.

"Apparently, he never removed me as his emergency contact after we got divorced."

I stared out of window as Neal weaved in and out of traffic. Deep down I knew Tony still loved me. The reason he wanted the hospital to contact me was because he wanted the only woman he ever truly loved there by his side.

"I'm sure he'll be alright, Ash. Tony is a strong, and healthy man."

"Yes, he is." I said as I choked back the tears.

Twenty minutes later, we stood at the admissions desk in the emergency room. The admissions clerk confirmed Tony had been admitted and was in surgery. She told us to take the elevator to the second floor and turn right for the trauma unit. I broke down and cried and Neal placed his arms around me. I prayed Tony would be all right, and at the same time, I could see the love for me in Neal's eyes.

The elevator doors opened and we walked down the hall to the trauma unit. The nurse looked up from her chart and pointed to the waiting area where I saw Tony's parents, his brother Derek, and Tony's partner, Garth. Despite the circumstance, they were surprised and glad to see me.

I walked over to Tony's parents and gave them a hug and introduced them to Neal. Tony's father, David, stood up and shook Neal's hand. I sat down next to Tony's mother, Louise, pulled a balled up tissue out my pocket, and wiped my tears. She patted my knee in a comforting way and said in her sweet southern accent.

"He's been in surgery thirty minutes."

"What happened?" I asked wiping my nose.

"He was working undercover; something drug related. There was a shoot out and Tony got hit twice. The good news is the bullets didn't hit any of his vital organs."

"That is good news."

Out of the corner of my eye I saw a tall beautiful woman I did not recognize but noticeably favored me. I turned my head to get a better look.

"Louise, who's that girl talking to Garth?"

Without blinking an eye, she said it was Tony's new friend Angelina. Then she changed the subject. "How are my grand babies doing?"

I dried my tears, wiped my nose, ran my fingers through my hair, and quickly pulled myself together. "Oh, they are fine." I said, opening my purse to remove my compact and apply a quick swipe of lip-gloss.

Louise chuckled. "Honey, don't you worry about that. They come and they go."

Embarrassed, I looked around for Neal and found him standing in the corner staring at Angelina's boobs.

"Neal!" I shouted, breaking his trance. Could you come here please?"

"Sure, Baby." He walked over and sat down. "What's up Baby?"

"Nothing," I said and I reached over and held his hand. He smiled.

Two hours later, the surgeon walked in with little emotion on his face. "The surgery was a success," he said.

There was a sigh of relief, and Louise and David hugged and gave praise to God. After the mini celebration, the doctor continued. "We removed the bullet lodged in his right hip. The other bullet passed through his right thigh muscle and missed the bone and any major artery. He is very lucky man and I expect him to have a full recovery. He is being moved to the intensive care unit."

"Thank you doctor," said David as he shook his hand in thanks.

"When can we see him?" Angelina asked.

"He is asleep, and will be out a few hours." Are you his wife?"

"No. I'm his girlfriend."

"I'm sorry," the doctor said. "Only immediate family can see him right now."

I grabbed Neal's hand. "We can go home now. Rachael and Michael will be glad to know he is all right. Thanks Neal, for being here for me. I love you."

"I love you too."

Chapter 18

*T*he next four years presented their share of normal challenges, and we managed to get through all of them without any major drama. The kids, now teenagers, were involved in sports. Quality time together over dinner happened once a week. To bring the family back together, I planned a family vacation to a theme park in Florida the week of our fifth anniversary. I hoped the trip would not only bring the kids together, but Neal and I closer. The week we were leaving, Neal came home every day in an irritable.

"Honey what's wrong? I have noticed lately you have not been your self."

"I'm fine, Baby. Just under a lot of stress at work."

"Do you want to talk about it?"

"No, I'll be alright."

"I think once we leave for our vacation, we will all be fine."

The day before our trip, I got up at 7 a.m. to do a quick load of laundry. I gathered my dirty clothes and made a small pile on the floor. I grabbed Neal's pants off the chair, checked his pockets, and pulled out two long white pills. *These do not look familiar.* I checked the prescriptions in the medicine cabinet. No match. I walked out of the bathroom and sat on the bed.

"Good morning, Honey." I rocked the bed enough to wake him up.

"Morning." He mumbled with his eyes closed.

"I found these in your pant's pocket. What are they?"

Neal opened his eyes to see me holding the pills close to his face. "Those are pain pills for my migraines. And why are you snooping through my clothes?"

I ignored the question. "You never told me you had migraines."

"Yes, I did."

"What kind of pain pill is this?" I asked, annoying him further.

"Oxycodone."

A wave of uneasiness washed over me and I had a flash back to the story of a former coworker who was addicted to Oxycodone. She lost her job, her home, and her husband.

"This is a prescription drug. Who gave it to you?"

"Why? You don't know him."

"That's not the point. If you are having headaches, why don't you go to the doctor?"

"I did go, and was told my headaches are caused by stress, take a couple of Motrin, and have a nice day. I don't have migraines every day; just every now and then."

"Is this why you've been acting anti-social? You could have told me, Neal."

"You're right. I'm sorry."

"Okay. Promise me, you won't take any more Oxycodone."

"I promise, I won't."

I kissed him and left the room feeling a little uneasy. Neal waited for me to reach the bottom of the stairs before he picked up the phone to call his friend.

"Hey, it's me. I'm going to need ten. I'll be there in an hour."

The following morning we boarded a plane to Orlando.

Chapter 19

*W*e returned a week later with a renewed sense of closeness. The kids were getting along better, and Neal's migraines had stopped. The following Saturday Neal and I were sitting in the kitchen having coffee when Joyce walked in.

"Morning Dad, morning Ashley," she said smiling.

"Morning," we said in unison.

Two minutes later Rachael walked in. "Morning, Mom. Morning, Neal."

"Morning," we said.

"What time are you girls supposed to be at volleyball practice?" I asked pouring more coffee.

"Practice starts at ten," Rachael said.

The phone rang and Neal answered it.

"Hello…," no answer. "Hello." He raised his voice.

I made eye contact.

"Hello Neal, this is Jackie," the voice said on the other end. A serious look crossed his face and I moved closer to him.

"What do you want?" he asked in a reserved, nasty tone. Joyce and Rachael stopped eating and listened.

"I know you are surprised to hear from me. I just wanted to

say I'm sorry, and I would not blame you one bit if you hang up," Jackie said, trying to say as much as she could in case Neal in fact, did hang up.

His grip tightened around the phone.

"I hope one day I can see my daughters again. Take care."

The call ended.

"Who was that?" I asked. Joyce and Rachael waited for his answer.

"I'll tell you later," he said in a daze. He sat his coffee on the table and walked out of the room.

I followed him into the bedroom and closed the door. "Who was that?"

"Jackie." He said looking down at the floor.

"What did she say?" After he repeated the conversation, we sat in silence. "Well, I had a feeling we would hear from her one day. Are you going to tell the girls she called?"

"No. They may become angry, or they may want to see her. I'm going to have to play this one by ear."

I let out a long sigh.

Chapter 20

*T*hree months later, the kids were home alone when the phone rang.

"Someone get the phone!" Janice yelled.

On the fourth ring Joyce answered. "Hello."

There was a pause before a female voice whispered, "Joyce?"

"Yes?"

"It's Mom."

"Mom!" Janice over heard her sister and leaped out of bed, and picked up the portable phone in her room.

"Hello! Mom?" Janice said with caution.

"Yes, Baby, it's me." Joyce's voice escalated.

"Where are you?" asked Joyce. Her voice trembled. Unable to hold back the tears she broke down. Janice ran down the stairs to comfort her younger sister.

Rachael and Michael stood at the top of the stairs and watched the drama unfold. The girls listened to the mother who had left them seven years ago. Joyce was ecstatic to hear from her, but Janice held fixed with her emotions as she listened. Five minutes later, the call ended.

Janice called her father at work. "Dad! Mom just called."

Neal frowned at the phone. "What did she say?"

"She said she was sorry and that she wanted to see us."

Neal remained silent.

"Dad?"

He was trying to be careful with his response; not wanting to show anger. "I'm here, Baby. How do you feel about that?"

"I'm pretty angry Dad, to be honest."

Neal took a deep breath.

"How's Joyce?"

"I'll ask her when she stops crying."

Neal's heart sunk. *Damn her!* "I'm on my way home. It's up to you whether or not you want to see her, Janice. I understand how you feel. Whatever you decide, I'm fine with it. We'll talk when I get home. I love you."

"Love you too, Dad."

Neal arrived home thirty minutes later and had a long talk with Janice and Joyce. In the end, they agreed to see their mother.

Later that evening, Neal called Jackie. He got right to the point when she answered the phone. "The girls agreed to see you, although I don't know why." He tried hard not to sound bitter. "I'm calling to make the arrangements. They are available this Sunday after three."

"Sunday will be perfect!" she said. While Neal could not see her, he knew she was smiling.

"Meet us at the Baltimore Harbor inside the gift shop near the elevator. And Jackie, if you don't show up, don't ever call us again."

"Okay, I understand. Neal, I know this isn't easy for you."

Neal ended the call without a response.

✳✳✳

The following Sunday, the entire family waited outside the gift shop at 3 p.m. Fifteen minutes later, Jackie had still not arrived.

"Let's go," Neal said sharply.

"No, let's wait a little longer. She could be running late. The kids are in the gift shop shopping. Let's give her fifteen more minutes," I said in a plea for a woman I had only heard the worse about.

Neal paused and folded his arms. "Alright, we'll give her fifteen more minutes and not one minute more."

Two minutes later we heard the elated screams of Janice and Joyce. Seeing the joy on the girl's faces sparked a twinge of jealousy. The ex-wife is back.

Chapter 21

At the end of August, Rachael and Janice left for their first semester in college. *Two down and two to go.*

Months passed and Neal and I drifted further apart. We lived under the same roof, slept in the same bed, and we only spoke to one another out of need. I had grown comfortable with that situation until he came home around 4 a.m.

He entered the bedroom and closed the door quietly. He eased in the bed being careful not to wake me. I pretended to be asleep. Ten minutes later he was asleep. After the first snore, I slipped out of bed, turned the bathroom light on, and searched through his pants, shirt pockets, jackets, wallet. I found nothing.

Frustrated, I sat on the bed and was staring at his dresser when I noticed a book on top of his dresser. *When did he start reading?* I walked over to the dresser and picked up the book. *The History of the Civil War. When did he become a military buff?* I opened the book and eight white pills sat inside of a perfect square hole in the middle of the book.

"Find what you're looking for?" his sinister voice made the hair on my neck stand up. He looked over my shoulder at the book.

"I…I thought you were sleep," I said as I turned around.

"No, my dear. How can I sleep when I hear you rummaging through my stuff? What are you doing with that book?"

I wanted to back up, but the dresser blocked my move. For the first time since I had known him, he frightened me. I positioned the book between us as a barrier. I then felt I had to put on an act of bravery. "You mean this book? I…I…"

He inched closer. "Give me the book!" His arm trembled and his eyes were dark.

I wanted to scream. I wanted to let go with an ear-piercing primal scream that would awaken the neighborhood. I took a deep breath, opened my mouth, and said, "Here!" I shoved the book into his chest.

He glared at me with dark evil eyes and said, "Let me be perfectly clear Sweetheart. I am not going to tolerate you going through my things, and don't let it happen again."

He walked over to the bed, placed the book under his pillow, and got into bed. "Good night, my dear."

I slept in Rachael's room.

Chapter 22

Monday I arrived to work and the office was buzzing with excitement. Ivy and Charlene appeared to be in a deep monologue in front of my office.

"What's going on?" I asked interrupting their conversation.

"It's official the Chicago Division One office is relocating to Baltimore. Six employees who worked in that office have opted to relocate to our Division.

"Do you know who's coming?

"Not yet, but we will know before the end of the week. The entire office is moving up to the fifteenth floor." Charlene said.

"Wow, it was finally happening. The rumors were true. I need a cup of coffee."

"Aren't you excited?" Ivy asked, confused by my lack of emotion to the news.

"Of course I am. I didn't get much sleep last night and I'm a little tired. When are we moving?" I asked, changing the subject.

"Before the end of the month. Movers stocked the main conference room with storage boxes this morning. Everyone has been ordered to start packing. Shireen is managing the move. We call her the Gatekeeper."

"Great," I walked into my office long enough to toss my purse on my desk before I joined Ivy and Charlene in the conference room.

"So what is up with you Ash?" Ivy asked.

"What do you mean?"

"You haven't been your usual happy self lately. How are the kids and Neal?"

"They're fine. Can you help me pack up 18 years of stuff?"

"I can, after you help me pack up 15 years."

"I asked first."

We grabbed as many boxes as we could carry back to my office. We filled the boxes with books and ceramic trinkets I had collected over the years. Ivy talked about the Las Vegas conference as she unpacked the file cabinet while I sat down at my desk and took a break. I opened the bottom draw to assess how much junk I had, and froze when I saw a photo of me and Tony that was taken in college. Fond memories flooded my mind as I stared at the photo. Two minutes passed, and I was still traveling down memory lane.

Ivy cleared her throat. "Ummm, Ash...Am I interrupting something?"

I looked up with a smile. "No, I was in the middle of a thought."

"And it looks like a very pleasant one."

I laughed. "I found a photo of me and Tony when we were 19 years old."

"Let me see."

"Wow, you were a handsome couple."

"Yes, we were," I said with a little sadness.

"Do you regret divorcing Tony?"

"Nope. We actually get along better now. The last time I saw Tony he invited me to join him and Michael for dinner, and I actually considered it for a second." I took a deep breath. "I can pack the rest of this stuff later Ivy. I'm done. Thanks for helping."

"We are not done yet. Let's check out our new office upstairs. I'll get the keys from the Gatekeeper."

Ivy darted out of the room. I kissed the photo and dropped it inside my purse. Two minutes later, we were on the elevator. The door opened and our eyes fell on a beautiful 200-gallon saltwater fish tank built into the wall in the reception area. It was filled with exotic tropical fish. There was plush seating and beautiful paintings of marine life, by local artist, that lined the wall. Tall tropical plants that were strategically placed around the room, created a warm tropical atmosphere. As we walked to our office, we stopped a few times and admired the watercolor paintings that line the wall that led to our office.

"Look. That is your office on the left. And mine is right next to you," Ivy said.

I unlocked the door and my mouth fell open. The entire back wall was floor to ceiling glass with a spectacular view of downtown Baltimore and the Harbor. The office was furnished in a modern contemporary style with an all-glass desk supported on curved steel gray legs. Two large steel-framed bookcases with glass shelves filled the right wall. I stood in the window for several minutes admiring the view.

"Are you ready to head back?"

"Nope," I said. "I'm ready to move today!"

"Me too! The view is spectacular! I'll be in my office when you are ready."

"Okay, I'll see you in a minute."

I spent a few minutes watching people go in and out of restaurants and wished it were me. I wondered how long I would be able to keep up the happy marriage façade. I locked the door, turned around, and saw Kyle Ayers' name on the door adjacent to my office. I smiled.

Chapter 23

*T*he Chicago Division One team moved to Baltimore at the end of the month. It had been twenty years since I had seen Kyle, and now he stood in front of the conference room introducing himself to the staff; more handsome now than ever.

"Is that the guy you told me about? The one you did the internship with?" Ivy whispered as she checked him out from head to toe.

I nodded yes.

"He is gorgeous. I mean… don't get me wrong, but how did you resist that?"

I looked at her and smiled. After the staff introductions, Kyle walked right over to me. I extended my hand for a handshake, but he moved my hand and smothered me in a hug. A warm tingling sensation raced through my body. It was a feeling I had not felt in years. We held our gaze for a moment then he smiled. Dimples appeared.

"Ash, how are you? It's great seeing you again. When I saw the name Ashley West on the program, I had no idea it was you. You are still as beautiful as I remember."

Ivy faked a cough.

Kyle released me slowly keeping his eyes fixed on mine.

"Are you all settled in?" I asked.

"At work, yes. At home, I'm renting until I find a house. How has life been treating you Ash?"

"Great. I'm married with four kids."

"Wow! Four kids?"

"Yeah, I have a son and daughter, and my husband has two daughters. And you?"

"I'm divorced, and I have a son and daughter. Ash, I have to go, Shireen is waiting patiently to speak to me. I'll see to you later."

"Okay, and it's great seeing you. I look forward to working with you again."

"So do I," he said. He smiled and walked out of the room.

"That's an interesting look on your face," Ivy said smiling.

I had forgotten she had been standing there the whole time. "Don't start Ivy. I'm married. Remember?"

"Yes, but that look in your eyes says, 'I wish I wasn't.'"

Chapter 24

Saturday morning I went into the office to work on my projections. I stepped off the elevator, into a silent corridor. Perfect. I can work *undisturbed*. Three hours quickly passed before I took a break. I took off my reading glasses and rubbed my eyes. I heard festive street music coming from somewhere, and swiveled my chair around to look out the window.

Happy people were walking along the pier, going in and out of restaurants, and all the while, I could not stop thinking how I was in a marriage from hell. I stood up and pounded my fists against the window and yelled, "It's not fair! I want to be happy too!" I fell backwards into my chair. I had been unhappy for so long that I had grown comfortable with feeling miserable. At that moment, I realized, I had made misery my friend. I called Laurie.

"Hello," she said in her usual busy-sounding voice.

"Hey girl, what's up?"

"Hey Ash, haven't heard from you in a while. How's married life treating you?"

"It's okay. I'm at work right now."

"On a Saturday?"

"Yeah, and…"

At the end of the hallway the elevator doors opened and Kyle stepped out. He headed to his office and noticed the door to Ashley's office was open. He unlocked his door to go in, but paused to eavesdrop on her conversation.

"I have something to tell you. Neal has not been coming home at night."

"What! Why?"

"Because he's cheating with his ex-wife."

"What! How do you know?"

"We had a big argument and he said some things that made me think he was seeing her. So, one night I drove by her house and his car was parked in her driveway!"

"Men are so stupid! Why would you park your car in the driveway?"

"Laurie, can I finish, please."

"Okay… okay…sorry, what happened?"

"I sat in the car and waited for him to come out."

"You what?"

"I waited for him to come out."

"Ash, I would have been out my car before I put it in park and…"

"Laurie! Can I finish?"

"Okay…okay, sorry. Damn…Go on."

"I sat there for a long time having back-to-back anxiety attacks. I was too scared to knock on her door, so I left." Tears welled up in my eyes and at the same time, I felt a sense of relief telling Laurie what happened.

"I'm sorry, Ash. Did you at least throw a brick through his window?"

"No," I wiped my tears.

"Slash his tires?"

"No." I blew my nose.

"Pour sugar in his tank?"

"No Laurie. Damn, I didn't know you had the 'hood' gene in you like that."

"How do you think I have stayed married eighteen years? I don't play! I'm sorry Ash. I feel bad because I introduced him to you. How long has this been going on and why didn't you call me sooner?"

"I didn't call because I feel like a fool."

Kyle had heard enough. He tiptoed back to the elevator and pressed the button. When the door opened, he whistled on his way down the hallway to his office in an effort to pretend he was just coming in.

"It's not your fault. He was a good man. I am so sorry you're going through this again."

"There's more," I said, letting the other shoe drop.

"Mercy! Girl, what?"

"He's addicted to Oxycodone."

"That's a very expensive habit. Is he paying bills?"

"Yeah, he is. And Tony is paying child support and trying to get me to come back to him. Wait, hold on a second, I think I hear someone."

I jumped out of my chair and looked out the door. It was Kyle. "Hi Kyle! What are you doing here on a Saturday?"

"I was just about to ask you the same thing," he said. "I have a couple of reports I need to work on before the Vegas conference. Why are you here?" he asked.

"Same reason; playing catch-up. Excuse me for a moment; I have someone on the phone."

"Sure, you know where to find me."

Kyle unlocked his door and entered his office. I returned to my desk and took Laurie off the speaker.

"Laurie, I have to go. I'm glad I told you because I don't know what to do. Part of me hopes the old Neal will come back. My kids think I'm crazy. I think Tony knows something is wrong because he keeps coming on to me, and the thought of going through another divorce is overwhelming. I have too much on my plate."

"Ash, you know I always advocate to keep families together and I would never tell you to leave your husband. And you are correct, you do have a lot on your plate. I can't believe Tony's trying to get back in the picture. Umm…Umm…Umm. Whatever you decide, you know I'm here for you."

"I know. And, thanks for listening. I'll call you later."

Two hours later I yelled, "Kyle, I'm done. I'm out of here!"

"I still have a couple of hours to go, Ash. The conference in Vegas is going to be long and boring, so I have to make my presentation exciting enough to keep people awake."

I grabbed my purse, locked the door, and walked into his office. "How do you know the conference is going to be boring?" I asked.

"Because my old division went to Vegas every year for an annual conference. I love Vegas, but I hated the conference."

"I have never been, but I always heard good things about Vegas."

"You're going to love it." He stared at me for a few seconds as if he had something he wanted to say, but changed his mind.

"Well, Ash, I'll see you Monday. Have a good weekend."

"You too Kyle."

Kyle waited for the elevator ding before he picked up his phone. "Hi, I would like to make a reservation for dinner please."

Chapter 25

*T*wo weeks later, on a rainy Tuesday morning, I arrived at the Baltimore Washington Airport to catch a flight to Las Vegas, Nevada. Ivy and Kyle met me at the gate, and four hours and three glasses of wine later we landed in Las Vegas excited, and feeling good.

We checked into the Paris Hotel, and stayed long enough to drop off our suitcases and use the restroom before we headed out to the strip. We walked along the strip, and stopped and watched the entertainment in front of every hotel along the way. We had lunch at the Bellagio, and dinner at Caesars. Kyle was right. I did love Vegas!

When we decided to call it a night, it was midnight Vegas time, but 3 a.m. Baltimore time. We returned to the hotel happy and exhausted. We got off the elevator on the tenth floor and headed to our rooms. Ivy stopped at her door. "See you all in the morning."

I nodded okay.

"Good night Kyle." I gave him a quick hug and thanked him for the tour. "See you in the morning." I said as I stood in the doorway.

"Good night Ashley. See you in the morning." Kyle said. He entered his room and stretched out across the bed. He regretted never telling Ashley how much he loved her. His last thought before dozing off to sleep. *This time Ashley, I'm not going to let you get away. I promise.*

I woke up with a hangover, and called Ivy for Aspirin. She knocked on my door in her bathrobe, handed me a bottle, and left. Forty-five minutes later, we walked into the conference with a 16-ounce cup of coffee. I looked around the room and was glad to see I was not the only one nursing a hangover. The only people who displayed any energy were the guest speakers.

An hour into the conference, the guest speaker came to the conclusion that there was no life behind the glazed looks in everyone's eyes, and initiated an unscheduled break. The room cleared in thirty seconds. Smokers raced out the door to the left, and coffee drinkers raced to the right to get more coffee.

The meeting ended around 4 p.m. I checked my phone for messages. No word from Neal. I took a deep breath to stop myself from getting an attitude.

"Okay Kyle, you are the official tour guide. What is on the agenda tonight?" Ivy asked with renewed energy.

"I got tickets to a concert that starts at seven. Let's meet in the lobby at six?"

"Sounds good, right, Ash?" Ivy noticed my sudden mood change.

"Yes, it does," I said and faked a smile.

"I'm going to make sure both of you have an unforgettable time tonight," Kyle said as he walked away.

Two hours later, Ivy and I waited for Kyle in the lobby. I wore black pants and a sexy off-the-shoulder black top. Ivy wore a silver sequenced tank top over black pants. My attitude went away after grazing at the buffet table. Carrot cake is my favorite comfort food. At 6 p.m., the elevator door opened and Kyle stepped out wearing navy blue slacks, and a tailored cream color shirt. He was holding two bouquets of flowers.

"Ladies, you are looking beautiful this evening," he said as he offered me his right arm, and Ivy his left. He handed us the flowers and escorted us to an awaiting limousine. Ivy and I exchanged glances. The chauffeur opened the door and we climbed in. Kyle sat between us, and as soon as the limo began to roll, he opened the mini bar and took out a bottle of champagne.

"What's the occasion?" I asked, holding my glass out for a fill.

"It's your first time in Vegas and I want it to be special. Ivy, this is your second time in Vegas and I want it to be special for you too."

He filled our glasses and we made a toast to Vegas. On our way to the theater, Kyle rolled down the window and pointed to a video billboard that showed Celine Dion performing. "That's where we are going!" he said.

I was speechless, and Ivy screamed in delight.

"Kyle, she is one of my favorite singers, thank you, thank you, thank you." Ivy bounced around in her seat like a child.

"How were you able to get tickets on such a short notice?" I asked.

"I have my connections," he said smiling.

Inside the theater our seats were in the second row from the stage. The moment Celine stepped on the stage we were mesmerized by her performance. I started to feel a familiar connection to Kyle and wondered if he also felt it. I never told anyone what happed that night in Chicago when we were interns. That was a life event that I will be taking to my grave.

After the show, we walked over to the Bellagio and watched the fountains dance to the rhythm of the music. Kyle and Ivy laughed and talked and my mind kept drifting to Neal. Everyone around me seemed happy. I cannot live the rest of my life feeling like this. I took a deep breath, and looked up at the stars. All the sounds and voices around me became mute, and a soft voice in my head confirmed my decision to divorce Neal.

At that moment, the sadness I had been carrying lifted like a boulder from my chest. In that same instant, my mood perked up. I returned to the hotel happy, tired, and broke. We stepped out of the elevator on the tenth floor thanking Kyle for a wonderful evening.

"Good night, Kyle and thank you again for everything," Ivy said as she swiped her card key and opened the door.

"You're welcome," said Kyle.

"Good night, Ash, and call me in the morning," Ivy said, singing one of Celine's songs as she closed the door.

"Okay," I said as I swiped my card and opened the door. For a brief moment, I looked at Kyle and wondered, *What if?* Kyle looked at me as though he read my mind.

"Kyle, I can honestly say, this is one of the most memorable evenings of my life. Thank you doesn't magnify how much fun I had tonight but I'm going to say it anyway. Thank you."

"You're welcome, Ash." I sensed he wanted to kiss me, but resisted. He walked over to his room, swiped his card, looked back, and said, "Good night," and closed the door behind him.

Chapter 26

*T*he next morning the conference started promptly at 9 a.m. We survived the first four hours of training through the power of caffeine. At lunch we asked Kyle what he had planned for us later.

"It's a surprise," he said, smiling.

"I love your kind of surprises," Ivy said. We laughed.

"I don't know how you can top last night," I said.

"You know I can't tell Eric how much fun I'm having without him. He would be so jealous," Ivy said, laughing like a schoolgirl with a secret.

I grimaced at the thought of Neal. Kyle caught it and stared at me for a moment. They knew something was up because I had not mentioned Neal's name the entire time I had been in Vegas.

After an awkward pause I said, "Well you know what they say Ivy? 'What goes on at the Paris in Vegas, stays in Vegas.' I'm sure whatever you have planned, we will love it."

The conference ended promptly at 4 p.m., and Kyle instructed us to meet him in the lobby in an hour. A limo picked us up, and this time it dropped us off in front of the Stratosphere Hotel. Again I was speechless. Ivy jumped out of the car pointing up at the revolving restaurant.

"No…Kyle, you didn't!" Ivy said throwing her hand across her heart.

"Yes, I did. And guess who has a reservation?"

Instinctively, I hugged Kyle. "You're the best!"

"Anything to make you happy Ash," he whispered back.

I felt ashamed that he was able to see how unhappy I was, and closer to him because of his compassion and efforts to make me feel better. We entered the Stratosphere and rode the elevator up 300 feet to the top. The restaurant doors opened to a spectacular view of Las Vegas.

A hostess escorted us to a booth. I sat next to Ivy, and Kyle sat across from us. She handed us a menu and announced our waitress, Lenore, would be with us shortly. We placed the menu down on the table and stared out at the panoramic view of strip. We ordered appetizers, drinks, and our entrées.

Kyle opened up a little more about his private life. He talked about growing up in New York, the demise of his marriage, his children, and the painful divorce—without saying one negative word about his wife. I reflected on how Neal was the total opposite. He never said anything nice about his ex-wife.

"What college do your kids go to?" Ivy asked snapping me out of my daydream.

"My daughter attends the University of Maryland, and my son, Cameron, attends Southern University."

"Nice. At least you can see your daughter on the weekends."

"Yeah, if I can catch up to her."

"What's her name?" he paused and looked at me.

"Ashley. Her name is Ashley," Kyle said.

I stopped chewing and Ivy did too. We both knew that was no coincidence.

"Ashley, huh? Wow, that's a pretty name right, Ashley?" Ivy said, kicking my leg under the table.

"Ouch, I mean, what a coincidence." I said. Kyle shifted his position and looked out the window.

"How did you come up with that name?" Ivy asked facetiously.

"My wife came up with it."

"Oh, I see." Ivy kicked me again, hard.

Lenore returned to the table with another round of wine. At the end of dinner we knew Ivy's whole life story. How she met Eric, how long they had been married, and what college her daughter, Keva, would be attending next year.

When it was my turn, I focused my conversation around the kids, and avoided mentioning Neal's name altogether. The sun had set and Vegas lit up like Christmas. We stared out the window in silence until Kyle broke the spell.

"This time tomorrow, we will be on our way back to Baltimore. So, tonight we eat, drink, and gamble. To Vegas!"

"To Vegas!" we cheered simultaneously. We tapped our glasses, consumed more wine, and after dinner, we gambled.

Chapter 27

"**H**ello. This is your 7 a.m. wake up call," the voice on the other end of the phone said. I don't remember how I got back to the room. My head throbbed, and I was afraid to lift it off my pillow. *Where did I put the aspirin?* I tossed the cover off of me and sat up. I looked down and noticed I was still wearing the outfit I had on last night.

I called Ivy. "Ivy, wake up!"

"What time is it?"

"Seven. We have to be at the conference at eight."

"Oh nooo! I can't do it; my head is killing me."

"Mine too. I am bringing you your Aspirin."

I found the bottle, tossed two aspirins in my mouth and washed them down with water. I grabbed the card key, walked out the room, and knocked on her door.

Ivy opened the door, and to my surprise she was wearing the outfit she had on last night. We broke out in laughter. Forty-five minutes later, we were back in the conference room for the last time...thanks to a 20-ounce cup of coffee.

"Ivy, what time does your flight leave?" I asked.

"Three o'clock."

"Why so early?

"I don't know what the hell I was thinking about when I made the reservation."

"My flight leaves at nine tonight, but I'm thinking about extending my stay for another day."

"I wish I could extend my stay, but I have to get home to hubby. Sometimes separation can be good; you know what I mean?" I nodded and smiled.

Kyle walked in looking refreshed and grabbed a chair and sat down. "Good morning ladies, did you sleep well?" he asked. "We must have because we slept in our clothes," said Ivy.

I asked him about his flight, and it turned out that we were on the same flight. I told him that Ivy's plane departs at three.

He looked at Ivy. "Why don't you call the airline and see if you can change your flight?"

"I'll see, but I don't think my husband would be happy if I did change it," she said.

"Ivy, if you like, I can give Eric a call on your behalf." said Kyle jokingly.

"Kyle, I was beginning to like you and now I'm not so sure," replied Ivy.

Kyle laughed and returned to his seat. After the conference, Kyle said he had one last surprise for us. "Meet me in the lobby in a half hour; and don't worry about dressing up," he said.

"Kyle I have to pass on this one. I have to finish packing, check out, eat, and get a taxi to the airport. And thank you again for everything," said Ivy.

She hugged Kyle goodbye and we headed back to our rooms. "Kyle is really a nice person. I am surprised you weren't tempted to kick Tony to the curb during your internship," said Ivy.

"I was in love with Tony and I have no regrets.

"I understand. But, what's going on between you and Neal?"

I looked away. "Come on Ash, you haven't mentioned his name once since we have been here, and I noticed the way you look at Kyle. He's definitely got a thing for you Ash."

I couldn't hold it all in any longer. I sat on the bed and told Ivy everything. I relived the hurt and pain all over again. When I finished, Ivy put her arms around me and handed me a tissue.

"I'm sorry, Ash. You are too nice of a person to be treated like that. What are you going to do?"

"I'm filing for divorce when I get back. I don't care what my family or friends will think any more.

Ivy glanced at her watch. "Well Ashley, our little therapy session is over. I know that sounds crude, but I say that with love. And besides, Kyle is waiting for you in the lobby, remember?"

"Oh my gosh, I've got to change. Give me a hug and I'll see you on the east coast. Have a safe flight."

"You too. See you Monday!"

I ran out the room, changed clothes and headed to the elevator. On the way down I used the reflective chrome doors as a mirror to make sure my hair was in place. The elevator announced the lobby floor and the door opened.

"Tony!"

TESTIMONIALS

"I was completely swept away by this book. The story line and characters are so believable; the life lessons, so instructive. The clever perspectives and humor are an invitation to read the next book in this series."
—D.F. O.T., MAOM, Schoolcraft, MI

"The author depicts Ashley Parks' approach
toward marriage with imagery and dialogue
so vividly that I readily recognized the behaviors.
This novel leaves you wanting to find out what
comes next!"
—C. Ben, Upper Marlboro, MD

ABOUT THE AUTHOR

The inspiration to write, *How to Recycle Husbands Every 10 Years*, began when her girlfriends started affectionately comparing her to Elizabeth Taylor, after a couple of marriages.

It took five years to complete the book, two years to come up with a title, and four hours to create this bio.

She resides in southwest Michigan with her husband.

—Minette Summers